Charlie Steel can write, no doubt about it. You will find no truer testament of a man who has mastered his craft, than with the title story of this book, **Desert Heat, Desert Cold**. Its main character, Sandy, beaten, robbed, and left to die, is determined to turn the tables on his would be killers. The story takes you on a trek across a hot and arid desert. The details of Sandy's slow and painful journey will leave you searching for a tall glass of cool water.

From the desert's scorching heat, to the bitter cold of a raging winter storm, in the story ***Mountain Man Comes Home***, Mike Pardee learns that "Grass is not always sweeter on the other side of the fence" as he finds that life in town, married to a woman who doesn't love him back, is more than he can take. Eventually heading back to his rustic mountain cabin, he finds what he had been searching for, in the middle of a blinding snowstorm.

Something in the Woodpile is a humorous tale about a packrat going about his business, as only packrats tend to do. When small, but important objects begin to come up missing, the accusations fly. It brings to light the ease we have as humans to accuse others when things are not as they should be, even before we have all the facts, and as you shall see, sometimes with disastrous consequences.

All of the stories are well thought out and masterfully written. I found them very enjoyable and easy to read.

Throughout this book I found a central theme that bound these stories together as a single unit. It's the theme of relationships. How we treat each other, react to each other, and especially how we handle ourselves, and our relationships as we deal with unusual situations and the pressures of everyday life.

Scott Gese, Publisher, Rope and Wire
(www.ropeandwire.com)

DESERT HEAT, DESERT COLD
AND
OTHER TALES OF THE WEST

DESERT HEAT, DESERT COLD
AND
OTHER TALES OF THE WEST

CHARLIE STEEL
Tale-Weaver Extraordinaire

CONDOR PUBLISHING, INC.
Lincoln, Michigan

DESERT HEAT, DESERT COLD
AND OTHER TALES OF THE WEST

Stories by Charlie Steel

1st printing August 2009
2nd printing November 2012
3rd printing February 2020

1st Kindle edition November 2012

*Illustrations by Gail Heath, Harrisville, Michigan

Library of Congress Control Number: 2020931011

ISBN-13: 978-1-931079-33-4

Condor Publishing, Inc.
PO Box 39
123 S. Barlow Road
Lincoln, MI 48742
www.condorpublishinginc.com

Printed in the United States of America

DEDICATION

This is a personal tribute to writers dead and gone who still live on through their writing and their books
—especially to—
James Oliver Curwood, Zane Grey, Max Brand, Louis L'Amour, and Jack London.

TABLE OF CONTENTS

DESERT HEAT, DESERT COLD

In my clouded brain I could hear their laughter. It echoed and rolled and would not dissipate. My head ached where they busted me with a pistol, and my sides pained from the kicks they gave me while I lay on the ground, helpless. They laughed and laughed as they kicked me, as if I were some child's plaything. I could hear Red say, "What a sucker!"

"Yeah," Whisky's voice echoed in my head. "The poor fool never suspected us from the beginning."

As I lay on the coarse desert ground, they continued laughing and kicking me until I passed out.

The first thing that came to life was my right hand and arm. I reached out and touched something; it was a rock—fiery hot in the intense heat of the sun. I quickly drew my hand back. Close to the ground it was probably more than 120° in this Mexican desert.

Slowly I regained all my senses. My head pounded with each heart-beat. My sides ached. With every breath a sharp pain tore through several of my ribs. I think they were cracked or broken. There were grains of sand in my left eye and they grated on my eyeball each time I blinked.

I was hot—burning up—but there was no sweat. The sun and heat took care of that. It sucked the perspiration dry before it had a chance to cool my body. I would die if I did not move and find shade.

I willed myself to get up. It hurt. Pain shot from my ribs and throbbing head. Sweat broke out on my forehead only to be quickly evaporated by the heat. I got to my knees and then slowly to my feet. I nearly fell back down. I staggered to a large rock and leaned against it. I looked around and saw nothing but bright sunlight and shimmering heat waves.

I surveyed myself and my surroundings. I had one or two broken ribs, a large gash in the back of my head, and I was sick and dizzy with the pain of it. My shoes and socks were gone; I had no jacket, no hat. Just my shirt and pants and what few possessions I had in my pockets: a small jack-knife, handkerchief, a couple of pesos, and a vial of sulfur matches. Of course my .45 was gone and as was my life savings, four hundred dollars in paper currency stuck inside the lining of the cartridge belt.

I looked around again. I shaded my eyes and stared at tracks in the sand. There were the tracks of Red, a big footed and heavy fellow, then of Whisky, a sawed off runt of a man, but fast—deadly fast—with a six-gun. Then there were the deep prints of the lone mule, the one animal that had survived the trip, and was now heavily laden with seventy-five pounds of gold. The tracks went north, straight for the border a good two hundred miles away.

I squinted and stared north into the bright landscape. All I could see were miles and miles of flat desert, shifting heat waves wavering in the air above the pastel browns, and beige of the land. There was some green, but it was green of cactus, and of the harsh rugged plant life of the desert. Not for fifty miles was there another water hole that I knew of. And that was straight north.

I reflected on it hard; I was a dead man. I might as well lay down and die. I looked for a larger rock and shade. Finding one, I staggered to the small shaded side, leaned against it, and slid down holding my head in my hands. It hurt, and each time I touched it, there was fresh gore and blood on my hands. I reached in my pants pocket and took out my bandanna—the one I used as a handkerchief. It was none too clean, but what was I to be fussy about? I wrapped it around the top of my sweat encrusted head. It covered the wound and warded off some of the heat of the sun that was frying my brain.

"Yup," I reflected out loud. "Sandy, you're a dead man."

I considered my options. Without boots, socks, water, or a gun, it was hopeless. Plain hopeless. Yet, I didn't want to die. Not now, not yet, not in my first twenty-one years of life. Besides, Old Bill, he didn't raise me to be no quitter. Old Bill would spit and punch me in the nose if he heard me talking this way. Maybe at second thought, he is here right now, by my side, helping me.

Wasn't it Old Bill who taught me everything I know? Wasn't it him who found me as a kid wandering the southern wagon trail west? Wasn't it him who took me in and taught me how to live off the land up in New Mexico? How to watch the animals at the water holes? How to catch em with or without a gun? How to cook the meat and preserve the hides? Didn't he teach me how to read trail, stay scarce from white man and Indian alike? To speak Spanish and his form of English?

I can hear him now. "Sandy, people are just no darn good. Ya jist can't trust none of em. You remember that! Don't you furgit er, no sir! When I'm gone, you'll learn it the hard way. Sure as shootin you'll go down to one of them crowded towns and look in a saloon and before ya know it, you'll be caught up in some mischief that will git you in trouble. Best thing to do, boy, is leave folks alone. Live up here, where you got all a God's creation to look on and not one lousy human being!"

"You were right, Old Bill. Too darn right!"

What was I going to do? Lay here and die in two days, or get up and try to save myself and get those two lousy skunks who bushwhacked me? Well, no use to feel sorry for myself. It was all my own fault. Just like Old Bill said, I went to a town and a saloon and I met these two jaspers who hired me to take them down here into the desert. They had a map and they pointed the way they wanted to go. I knew the desert, the water holes—and the thousand dollars they offered me was a lot of money. I should have known better. They said they were after gold and a lost mine. Yeah, it was gold alright—two strong boxes of Mexican coin—about $45,000 dollars worth.

Well, if I was going, I better do what I could for my feet. It was going to be a long, painful, bloody march over hot sand and sharp rocks. I took my belt off. At least I had that. I took the jackknife and cut the belt into two equal pieces. I wrapped a piece of leather around each foot and tied it together at the top with torn and rolled strips of my shirt sleeves. I got up and started walking north.

The first ten steps I thought I was going to faint, but I didn't. The next twenty I thought my ribs would come through my sides, but they didn't. The next fifty my head throbbed so bad, I thought it would explode and I would die right there, but it didn't and I kept on walking—if you could call the half-gated, staggering steps I took, a walk.

I reflected on some of the stories Old Bill told me. Whoppers they were. About men who were scalped by Indians and left for dead, but who jumped up alive and lived and fought to avenge their comrades' death. About pioneers and mountain men who starved or got frozen feet—who amputated their own toes. Who survived broken bones, and wounds that no natural human being should. How they went on to save others and do great deeds, and live long lives. The short of it being that, given the will, some men had lived while others had died. Men who should have died kept on against all odds. What's a gash on the head and bare feet compared with those before me?

"I hear you, Old Bill. I'm not giving up yet."

So, with Old Bill harping in my mind, I marched, walked, staggered—whatever you call it—thinking just one more step, just one more step. Time passed, and I went into a sort of trance, and my desert and mountain training kept me on course, straight north.

I was in great shape. Not an ounce of fat on me. I kept going and with it I captured time and distance. I actually think my muscles loosened up. The cracked ribs either pained me less or I got used to them. My head still throbbed but not like before. I was dizzy though, and groggy. Who knows, maybe that helped too.

I tried to step gingerly but occasionally I would come down on some unprotected part of my foot. Eventually the rocks cut at my heels and I could feel blood. I tried to ignore that pain, too. Bloody feet were part of the ordeal. I was not the first person to do this. It was either keep moving or die.

I didn't have much of a plan—but it was a plan. Red and Whisky were thieves. Lazy thieves at that. They would not go far today. Maybe I could out-distance them. I was afraid to overpower the two of them at night, or sleeping, but maybe, if by tomorrow I got to the water hole first, there would be a way.

The fluid in my body was drying up. Fast. The skin around my face was becoming tight; it felt hard and wrinkled. My mouth was dry, there was no saliva, and my tongue felt like a hard leathery hide. It hurt to breathe and sometimes I nearly choked from the increasing constriction of my throat in the dry air. This was what it was like to die in the desert heat.

With the loss of water, I was losing weight and my pants kept falling low around my hips. Every twenty steps or so, I would have to hike them up with my hands. After a long while, I faltered even more and began to fall to my knees. Several times I fell hard on the flinty rocks and they tore my pants and my skin. Blood was running down my pant legs and turning stiff. With each step I left flecks of blood in the sand from my torn feet. Worse, my drawers chafed a sore spot on my butt. The cloth became stiff and hard from the dry sweat. How I hated to go without a wash down. Old Bill used to tease me about that! Used to call me a doggone beaver, the way I liked to bathe.

I tried to smile at that thought and my lips cracked more, my bottom lip split in the middle and I tasted the blood. I sucked on it, taking some small relief from my own warm red fluid.

I trudged. I staggered. I swayed. I limped. I walked. I dragged myself along, willing each step—thinking that with each one I would fall and die, but I didn't. The dry hot air whistled through my lungs, it hurt to breathe.

Again I fell hard on my knees, cutting them against small jagged rocks. I cursed. I lay there exhausted, thinking it was impossible. I would never make it.

Something in front of me obscured my vision. For a long time I just stared at it. It wasn't a rock. It was funny shaped. Finally my breathing came easier and I focused. It was a boot! My boot! The darn fools must have thrown my boots up on the mule's pack. Being lazy, they didn't tie them down. If one boot fell, maybe the other would.

I was walking all this time on their very trail. I hadn't thought of it, but now it was important to remember. Had I missed the other boot? No! I would have seen it.

I dragged myself to a sitting position and reached for my soft worn leather boot. It was the right. I tore the front lower part of my shirt off and then unwrapped the leather belt from my bloody right foot. I cleaned off some of the clinging sand and carefully wound the piece of cloth around my bloody heal. The cloth stuck to the wet mess. Then I pulled the boot over my right foot.

I staggered to my feet and began to walk. Both feet hurt, but it was so much easier with my right foot in the boot. I picked up some speed and continued. Maybe the other boot would drop. For the first time that day I had hope and something to look for.

Then it began all over again—the pain of each step, each breath, each movement in the dry desert heat. My joints felt like they needed to be oiled, my sides gave out sharp pains, and my head throbbed. Still, I continued. Each step was a willful effort of pain, but it was either that or lie down and die. And that, I was not going to do.

I didn't bother to look at the trail; I tried not to look ahead; I just stared at the ground. It was enough to force each step. Somewhere in the pain of it all, I went into another trance. In it I kept walking north along their trail, almost oblivious to time and pain. I became this machine-like thing. The only thought was move, step, walk—don't stop.

Eventually, I began to fall again. With each fall my knees were cut more and each time it was harder and harder to get up. Finally I stopped. I tried to look up and into the distance but all I saw were dark wavering heat waves and blinding bright light. I looked down at the tracks plainly visible in the sand. That was my only reality.

At some point the light began to lessen and with it the heat. The sun was beginning to set. More hope. Then I thought of the cold. At night the temperature would drop sixty degrees and it would become freezing cold. With no clouds there was nothing to keep the heat from rising straight up and the cold from penetrating and falling down from the night sky.

My right foot got caught up in something and it dragged along. I looked down at it and stared. It was the other boot! The fools! Now I had a chance. I sat down heavily and took the leather belt from my left foot. As I had done with the right foot, I cleaned the bloody heel of sand and tore off and covered the cuts with another piece of cloth from my shirt. I then carefully put on my left boot. From somewhere I got the energy to stand up. I began to walk. It was better. Perhaps now I really had a chance.

The sun was setting fast. The air cooled. This was my favorite time of the day in the desert. For the next two hours the falling temperature would feel good. There would come a time when the temperature would be perfect and the body would be energized by it. Then, even as it cooled further, the ground gave up the last of its heat, enough to keep me going for several hours before it got really cold.

I marched along making much better time in my boots. As the heat dissipated my breathing became easier and my gait faster. Finally it went dark and the moon began to rise. The stars were out and I looked up. Millions of twinkling points of light flickered high above the desert, enough to light the ground. Even the white of the Milky Way was added to the glittering diamonds of the clear sky.

I began to feel more alive. My body was no longer losing moisture. I kept looking up the trail. I now had the strength to do that. I was staring at this one bright star low down against the dark horizon. Then it struck me; that was no star! Those lousy curs had stopped and built a fire!

Idiots! That fire could be seen for twenty miles. It could bring Apaches, Yaquis, and banditos of all sorts. They were not only lazy thieves, but stupid ones. No doubt they lit the fire for hot coffee and beans. There they sat with $45,000 in gold and they were announcing it to the entire country.

On the way down I had not let them light a fire, except during the noon hour. That was the only time we had hot coffee and beans. The rest of the time we ate and drank cold or chewed on jerky. Oh, if only I had a big cup of cold coffee to drink now! With my throat and tongue so dry, I am not even sure if I could swallow.

Well, at least I knew where those murderin' hombres were. But then, so did everyone else in the area. I wondered who would get to them first. Me or someone else? I wasn't going to walk up to their fire. I had no weapon and they would see or hear me coming. I wondered if they were smart enough to unload the mule and wet its nostrils and give it something to drink. No doubt, they would let the mule stand there and they would meet their needs first. I knew how they acted. Fools! The mule was the most important thing they had. Without it, they would not get the gold out. If they did not take care of it, the animal would not survive the desert.

As the air cooled, I felt better and my momentum picked up. I tried not to dwell on it but I had walked no more than twenty miles—less than three miles an hour for seven hours. I had about ten more hours of cool night and dawn before the sun would be back up. How far could I walk in ten hours?

I decided to skirt around their fire and head straight to the water hole. Would I make it? In time? And if I did, what could I do against two armed men—one of them a pistolero?

I picked up speed. I had thirty more miles to go. I could just make it if I didn't stop or fall or give up. Now that the temperature had dropped I felt much better. I could breathe and move easier. Perhaps I had a chance. I began to picture the waterhole and the plants that grew around it. I thought of an idea. First, I would quench my thirst, then soak my dehydrated body. After I would make a weapon and find a place of ambush and wait. Waiting around a water hole was dangerous. All the animals came to drink there including the cougar—and worse, the ones on two legs.

The full moon came up and brightened the desert. With the bright stars behind it, it was almost as light as day. My body made a shadow as I walked along. And I did walk and walk and walk. It was the first time I ever tried such a foolish thing. If only I had my horse. But it had died of thirst way back there. Unlike Red and Whisky, I could not bring myself to eat its flesh.

* * *

Red looked across the fire at Whisky. "Say, you reckon he's dead by now?"

"Nawwww, but I bet he wishes he was."

Both men laughed heartily.

"Say, Whisky, since you're up, pour me another cup of coffee."

"Red, I told you about that kind of stuff. I'm nobody's lackey. You want coffee, you git it yourself."

The mule stood by the fire, heavily laden with its two chests of gold. It had its head down, too weary to beg for water.

* * *

I came up near the fire before I knew it. I could see the mule standing there with its chests of gold still on its back. The poor beast. These men weren't fit to live. I was tempted just to walk straight in. I knew I could kill one of them but not both. When it did come time, I would have to take Whisky first. He was the one who would be hard to kill and the most dangerous. I kept on walking and took one last look at the fire as I went by. It was the hardest thing I ever did in my life and I was still not sure I could do it—walk another thirty miles through the night without rest, food, or water. Still, it was my only chance. If I stopped now, it would be over. In just another eight hours the sun would be up and it would suck the rest of my life from me. To walk through the night was my only chance.

Again I focused on the ridiculously simple task of raising one foot and putting it in front of the other. But it was not ridiculous, it was to save my life, and it certainly was not simple. No longer did I sweat. Now I was beginning to shake from the cold and it was getting colder. I trudged along and even tried to increase my speed to warm me. Every nerve, every fiber in my body screamed for rest, for water, and for food. My stomach was eating at itself now, but still I pushed myself forward.

I don't know how many times I stumbled, how many times I fell, how many times I cut my hands and knees on sharp rocks, but I did. Still I got up and kept going. Hours later, I found myself coming out of a type of trance—a walking trance. I must have looked like some kind of wounded animal. The pain was unbearable, but I refused to stop. I knew if I did, I would never get started again.

I looked at my lacerated hands. I put part of my right palm into my mouth and sucked on the blood. My dry tongue and mouth barely felt the hot liquid. When I swallowed I nearly choked. Every breath whistled in and out of my lungs and up my windpipe. I was beginning to think that this was the way I would die—walking. That I would fall one more time and never get up.

I did not know what kept me moving. There was no residual strength left. I was completely sick from dehydration, from lack of water, from no food or rest. I was dizzy, my head ached, and my ribs felt like they were coming through my sides with each breath I took.

It was starting to get light. The sun was rising. Already the air began to warm. I walked doubled over now. My instincts for direction had kept me on the right path. I forced my tortured body to straighten up. I looked north. A few miles ahead I recognized land marks, a small cliff and the knoll which hid the water hole. I actually stood up straight and began to walk faster. I was going to make it!

By the time I reached the water hole, the sun had been up for two hours and already it was beginning to get hot. The water hole itself was a large pool. From somewhere in the ground, a cold fresh spring bubbled up and fed this ancient water hole. The remarkable part about it was there were tiny pan fish that lived in it—fish that had survived from some other era when this ground had been covered by water.

I didn't stop when I came to the water hole. In fact, I couldn't. I just sort of walked straight in and fell down in the deliciously cold pool. I opened my mouth and the water actually burned my tongue, and my throat. It hurt terribly when I tried to swallow. But swallow, I did. Not too much water at first. My tongue felt like a swollen and rough piece of leather in my mouth. I don't know how long I laid there with just my nose and mouth sticking above the water, but I finally pushed myself up and dragged my body close to shore.

I lay in the shallow water for a long time. My body sucked up fluid from the outside and inside. Finally, the cold water sent a chill through my baked body and I stood up and sloshed out.

I knew I couldn't rest yet. I was too weak. I would have to have food if I were to over-power those two later. I needed to make a throwing stick, set snares, and make a spear. I set about all three tasks. I made snares on rabbit trails coming in through the grass to the water hole. I used rolled pieces of shirt for the snares. From a paloverde tree I cut off a limb that had four branches in opposing directions, sort of like a cross, and then sharpened all four ends for a throwing stick. From a type of cactus plant that put out one long shoot like that of a wooden staff with a flowered tassel, I cut a six foot pole. Then I began looking around for a hiding place—one that would allow me to ambush.

I was in my element now, thanks to Old Bill. I laid down above the pool and waited for game. Two plump doves flew in and I threw the stick. Too slow, I missed. I was out of practice. I waited again. This time a blue quail walked in, then another, and another. I threw the stick at one, missed and hit another. I popped up and ran for the wounded bird. I got him by the neck and twisted. I carried him a long way from the pool and started a very small but hot fire between rocks. Within a few moments I had the quail eviscerated, skinned of its feathers, and propped on a stick cooking. I could barely wait for it to be done. One time I picked it up and took a bite of raw hot meat. It burned my mouth and I cursed. After that I waited, and when it was done and cool, I ate. It was one of the most delicious meals I ever had.

I felt stronger. My stomach felt full, as if I had eaten a feast. I could feel the water rolling around in my belly and yet I went back to the pool for another drink. I was tired. My body ached, but I couldn't stop yet. I sharpened the tough cactus stalk into a spear point and then lit another quick fire and hardened it in the flames.

Next I gathered dry grass and constructed a sort of blind, not above the pool, but down beside it and on the far eastern edge. I had to be near enough to jump out and surprise those two men.

I heard something jumping about in the bushes. It was one of my snares. I ran over and clubbed a rabbit with a rock. As I knew it would, the rabbit had all sorts of vermin on it. I carried it by its ears and threw it where I had lit a fire and cooked before. I returned to the blind I had been working on and, when I had finished it, I placed my throwing stick and spear inside. I then went back and made another fire and singed the hair off the rabbit and watched as the vermin, all kinds of lice, jumped off or were burned in the flames. After that I pulled the fur off, disemboweled it, and cut it up and put it on sticks for cooking. When I was done, I ate one quarter of the rabbit and saved the rest for later. I then went back to my lair and lay down. The one thing I worried about the most, was would I be awake by the time they arrived. Another concern was if anyone else would show up at the water hole. These were my last thoughts before I fell stone cold asleep.

I should have had more discipline, but I didn't. Old Bill would not have fallen asleep at the crucial time. At least in all his stories, true or false, no one had ever gone to sleep in the moment of final climax. But I did. I was lucky Whisky and Red didn't come up on me and shoot me. Instead, I was awakened by a combination of splashing, laughing, and a mule braying.

I peered wearily through the grass hideout and saw both of the men trying to pull the stubborn mule from the waterhole.

"Get him out of there!" bellowed Red. "He'll drink too much and it will kill him."

"You blasted fool, what ya think I'm trying to do!"

I tried to move. Sharp pains went up my back and down my legs. I was stiff as a board. I attempted to get to my knees but my body just wouldn't work. I laid back down and tried to get the circulation going. I couldn't be stiff like this if I was going to over-power them.

The one thing I had told those fools over and over on the way down was that you approach a water hole quietly, get your water and get out. Since the spring could be a meeting place for all types of people, if you wanted to keep your hair, you did your fires and cooking elsewhere.

Right in front of the water hole Red and Whisky made this big old fire. They hadn't learned a thing. Well, it gave me time to get limbered up. I rose quiet like from my hidey-hole and just sort of tippy-toed right down to the fire. Both men had their backs to me. I just couldn't do it cold-blooded.

"Howdy boys," I said.

They both jumped up like snakes and turned. Whisky almost had his gun out when I thrust the spear into his chest right where his heart should be. I gave it all I had and I do believe that spear went all the way through and out his back. I followed the spear down and grabbed Whisky around the neck. Still standing, I turned him in front of me towards Red. Red began pumping bullets into Whisky's body while aiming for mine. I reached down and grabbed Whisky's six-gun and began firing back at Red. He had no shield.

Just like that, it was over. Red died first with three bullets to the heart. Whisky died a few minutes after with slugs in his legs and torso and that spear sticking out of his back. I stared at them a long time, before I noticed blood dripping from a gunshot wound in my left side. I finally went to the mule and pulled those darn gold boxes from its back. I swear that mule gave me a thankful look as it went to go pull and eat at grass.

*1st Printing, *THE SHOOTEST,* September/October 2007

MOUNTAIN MAN COMES HOME

"All you do is complain, woman!"

"Put your feet down off of that chair! If you was married to yourself, you'd complain too."

"Awe, it's more than a man can take."

"What man? I don't see no man around here!"

"That's it! Keep it up woman and I'll go!"

"You've been saying that forever and you're not gone yet!"

"Well, a man can only take so much."

"You'll take it and a sight more, I venture."

"What's for supper, woman?"

"I didn't fix it. I'm not hungry and tonight you'll do without!"

"That's the last straw!"

People had warned Mike Pardee that she was the town spinster for a reason. One man Mike clipped with a fist told him she was a shrew. Mike had come from the mountains and was a homely, lonely man. He met the woman at a town dance. They kept company on weekends and she made him manager at a stable she owned. When Persimmon Wilcox asked him to marry her, he accepted.

"You won't leave me, you're not man enough!" she shouted.

The packing didn't take long. There wasn't much that was his, just the clothes he brought with him. Percy Wilcox Pardee made him leave everything she had bought or given. Mike hated to fail at anything, and he was a dejected man when he left the big house. Word whispered around and the people of the small mountain town turned out to witness his departure. He took his two mules and left Trinidad in the same condition as he was before, a sad, lonely, and homely man.

Despair was no stranger to Mike Pardee, but humiliation was a new experience. Seeing the stares of the neighbors and people who watched his departure, made Mike vow that once again he would leave civilization and live alone. Perhaps he wasn't meant to be around human beings.

Getting back to the mountain cabin was a long climb of several days. His little cabin in the mountains was a welcome sight, tangible evidence of a former life. Once he had run away from it and now he was returning. Three years before he was eager to leave and now he was eager to come back. Mike learned that grass was not always sweeter on the other side of the fence. In this case, it was a bitter taste and one he wanted out of his system.

He walked up to the cabin eagerly, the shutters were closed and the door stuck tight. These he worked on for some time, then hauled in his supplies. He had a new .44 Winchester and a large number of shells. This would make his life much easier than using the old heavy bore war musket. Now he could fire at game and, if he missed, he had a chance at several repeat shots. There were elk, mule deer, and sometimes antelope. The buffalo were gone, but wolves, coyotes, beaver, and other animals remained. He would go back to being a trapper and a mountain man, and live as he had before.

His wife had made fun of his mountain skills and she humiliated him at every chance she could. When he ran her stables, Mike was paid little of what he was worth. A mere twenty five dollars a month, yet he was able to save most of it. Seven hundred dollars would keep him a long time and he turned it into gold coin and hid it away for the future.

Mike found himself humming and his disposition changed for the better. It was a relief to get away from the noise of people, and their flapping mouths. The stinging jibes from his wife would take longer to forget. In the morning the trapper awoke and came out from under his blanket of heavy furs. The stone floor was cold, and he made a mental note that a bear hide would make a good rug.

The old iron stove after three years of disuse was still capable of heating the cabin and cooking food. Wood would have to be cut and stacked. It would be a long cold winter and he needed plenty of fuel. It was this task he started first. He took the mules, put on two packs, one containing axe and saw. For the next week he cut and hauled pine logs. Then he spent another week sawing and splitting the logs. The wood was stacked in a lean-to.

Next he scythed and gathered enough grass for winter feed for the mules. This he stored in a shed that would double for a shelter for the mules. Through the remaining months of late summer and fall, Mike laid out his traps, tanned hides, and went trout fishing. Some of the meat he salted and dried. In October he shot a fat bear. He tanned the hide, rendered the fat and smoked the meat. The thick fur made a soft rug for the cold stone floor.

Soon the snow would come and it would be time to hunt elk and hang enough frozen meat to last the winter. Mike was a hard worker and he enjoyed all the physical toil. He took new pride in his skills. Before, he had thought little of his abilities, but now he knew no one else in that town could survive through a mountain winter.

During the past weeks Mike had watched a herd of nearly three hundred elk, feed, and roam across high mountain valleys. What he wanted was to take down a big bull close to the cabin. To cut and haul hundreds of pounds of meat would not be an easy job. He wanted to keep the hide intact and that too would weigh a great deal. It would take several trips and he would have to cache the meat, to keep it from scavengers.

For three days Mike sat on a high summit looking down over a green meadow and small rushing stream. It was cool, sometimes cold in the morning, but by afternoon it warmed up. He sat comfortably and enjoyed the sights that extended out before him. Over him was the large blue dome, pierced by jagged peaks rising nearly three miles up into the sky. Green carpets of thick grass rolled away before him, and on the slanted mountains grew the darker pines. In the valleys the shimmering leaves of quaking aspen turned yellow and stood out against the smooth white trunks of the trees. By staying hidden, the mountain man was entertained by foxes that made their quick, nervous, dainty-footed run as they chased after mice and ground squirrels. Buzzards floated on thermal currents, along with bald eagles. Hawks soared above and made their piercing scream. Below, deer, ever alert, grazed; coyotes hunted in packs, yipped, and screamed out their coded calls. Twice, Mike got a glimpse of a cougar, one lone wolf, and a mother bear and her cubs. Lesser game, including birds, came to drink and bathe in the clear waters of the little stream. This was the reason Mike had spent most of his years in the mountains. Now he regretted ever leaving it. He smiled to himself and knew that for the rest of his life, it was here he would remain.

Many miles away, Mike saw movement. It came from a high notch between two mountain peaks. At first it looked like game, but the forward movement was too steady. It could be a group of wild horses. It took hours before he identified three riders. Mike watched them curiously. It was unusual to see travelers in these high mountains at any time. Close to winter like it was, it was dangerous going. A storm and snow could come, and without shelter a person would die.

This used to be Ute country. Whites pushed the natives west out of fertile Colorado land. Perhaps the three below were Indians looking for a better place to live. The riders finally came into the green valley where Mike Pardee was hunting. The three stopped at the stream and dismounted. Mike could see that they were Utes; two of the riders were young and the third was injured. They were wrapped in blankets. The two younger Indians made a bed in the grass and helped the third rider to lie down. They made a fire and hobbled their horses. Mike watched from his high perch and did not move until dark.

Back at his cabin he reflected on what he saw. They were mighty poor Indians. They had no weapons or shelter of any kind that he could see. They would have a cold camp and if it stormed as he expected, by tomorrow there could be three feet, or more, of snow on the ground. Already the wind was whipping around and the temperature was dropping. Mike added wood to the stove throughout the night, and he kept warm in his tight cabin, despite the storm.

In the morning the wind was still blowing and with it, drifting snow. Mike found his old winter buffalo coat and snowshoes.

Reluctantly, he took his rifle and one of the mules. It might be dangerous to approach the three Indians, but it would be a sin to let them freeze to death. With some urging he got the mule to struggle through the snow. One time he had to shovel a drift open. They climbed over the mountain pass and down into the next valley. The Utes' fire was still burning and two younger Indians were huddled over the third. Mike approached cautiously.

"Maiku!" hollered Mike over the howling wind.

It was the only Ute word of greeting that he knew. He followed this up with raising his right hand.

In a few hours the snow would bury the pass and most certainly all four would freeze.

"We must go!" the mountain man shouted.

He followed in sign language. Coming closer, the white man saw that the two young Indians were boys. One was under ten years and the other a young man no older than fourteen. The person under the blankets was a woman and she could do no more than rise up for one look and then feebly fall back to her cold bed of snow covered blankets. Mike dismounted and without asking, picked up the woman and placed her upon his mule. He signaled for the boys to follow. They gathered their three bony horses and began to trudge through the snow.

Mike Pardee went before the mule and its passenger and dug a path through the deeper drifts. The two Indian boys followed. They struggled across the meadow and up the mountain pass. The three ponies refused the steep climb. They stood exhausted in the snow and were too weak to follow. The Indian boys gave up pulling on their reins, removed their halters, and left the horses behind. It was a long climb up and over the pass.

The wind had blown the snow clear at the top. On the cabin side of the mountain the drifts were not so deep. The woman straddled the mule. Mike had to hold onto her as they struggled through the snow. The boys did their best to follow. They fell often, and had difficulty coming to their feet. Mike took a rope and tied it to the neck of the mule and the other end to the two boys' waists. In this manner they were pulled along. The storm seemed to increase in its fury. The wind blew harder and just before they reached the cabin it became a complete whiteout.

In the blinding snow they missed the cabin but came upon the shed. The entrance was blocked by a huge drift.

Digging with the shovel the shed door was cleared and opened. The mule was pulled in along with the woman and two boys. Sheltered from the wind, it was instantly warmer. The mountain man lifted the woman gently and placed her on a pile of hay. He put the mule in a stall, wiped it down, and covered it with a blanket.

Taking a lariat, Mike forced the shed door open, stepped out, and pulled it closed behind him. He tied the rope to an outside post and disappeared into the swirling snow. The first time he came to the end of the rope and did not find the cabin. Holding onto the end of the line he turned to his right and bumped into the wooden building. He found the door nearly buried in the drifting snow. Tying the rope to a hitching ring he followed it back to the shed. Handing the wooden shovel to the oldest boy, he pointed to the cabin. The mountain man picked up the woman, covered her head with a blanket and carried her outside. He made sure the shed door was closed tightly then he followed the boys along the rope.

Mike signaled for the boys to dig out the cabin door. They were nearly frozen with exhaustion and cold. Laying the woman in a blowing drift, Mike took the shovel and dug frantically. After several attempts he was able to jerk the frozen door open. As quickly as he could he pushed the two boys inside and then carried in the woman. He laid her on his bunk and rushed to start a fire in the cold iron stove.

The female was not sick, she was wounded. A bullet had passed through her upper right shoulder. It had gone all the way through without striking bone. The rear exit wound was large and a lot of blood lost. The Ute woman was attractive. So were her boys. They were cold, weak, and starving. For more than a week the mountain man was not sure any of them would survive.

By the second week the boys were on their feet and helping in the care of their mother. Mike learned their Ute names were Ouray and U-re. He never got the gist of their mother's name. It sounded something like Nicky and that was the name he gave her. Nicky lay in Mike's bunk too weak to move. He spoon fed her broth while the boys watched his every move.

Mike put out paper and pencils in hopes of distracting them. Eventually they began to draw. They drew many violent pictures. From those, Mike was able to understand what they had endured.

Their village was attacked by gold hunting whites who burned and destroyed their shelter and their supply of winter food. Horses were killed, the men, women, and children butchered. Only a few escaped and they were chased down and murdered.

Ouray pointed at a series of sketches that showed how he gathered three ponies and led them west through the mountains and away from the killers.

"Whites crazy," managed Ouray in broken English.

The boy's eyes flamed when he said it. Mike managed a nod in agreement.

"I live alone," answered Mike. "I am white, but I will be your friend."

Ouray, the oldest turned away. U-re thumped his brother on the back and spoke angrily to him in fluid Ute. Then he pointed to his mother and the bed. After much discussion the younger boy turned to Mike and said a Ute word Mike understood.

"Tog'oiak," said the boy slowly.

He repeated the word and pointed to the cabin, the food, the warm stove, and his mother. The word meant thank you.

The first storm didn't last. There came another warm spell. Some of the snow melted and then froze. A hard crust formed and enabled Ouray and Mike to go hunting. Mike gave the Indian boy his old musket and together they brought down two elk. This they cut up and, with several trips, were able to put away over a thousand pounds of meat, enough to last them through the long cold winter.

Beds were made for the boys and himself, and skins were tanned for blankets. It took nearly a month before the woman was up and around. Then a daily routine set in. Mike began to teach them English and he learned a little more Ute. They played a game of pick-up sticks and when the weather permitted went out to hunt in the snow and get exercise. The woman took over the cooking and the meals improved. Before spring, all four came to know each other well.

Mike knew he was a homely man. Nicky was much different than his former wife. She spoke seldom, never nagged, worked diligently, and was kind to her two boys. In games of pick-up sticks she became intense and excited. She was dexterous and able to beat all three males. When she accidentally nudged a stick she groaned in dismay and then laughed in a funny little giggle.

When spring came and the snow melted away, grass

began to grow. Mike knew he had some kind of affliction. It was certain that the woman and her two boys would leave. For half a year Mike had the benefit of good company. It was the most pleasant six months he had ever spent. His loneliness and sadness had disappeared, and the thought of them going away made him sick inside.

There came a day when the boys went off fishing. Nicky was cutting meat for another meal and Mike worked at his traps.

"The air warms, all living things come," said the Indian woman. "Soon it will be time to go."

"When will you leave?" asked Mike.

"Soon. We must find our people. The boys must learn our ways."

"What if you cannot find them?"

"We must try."

"I…" attempted Mike and then dropped his head.

He got up and rushed outside. Mike picked up an axe and began cutting and splitting wood. He was angry and upset and he kept at it a long time. When he stopped he saw Nicky staring at him. During his attack on the woodpile she had placed food on an outside table and poured the last of the coffee into two cups. She was sitting on a bench and staring at him.

"You are angry," said Nicky.

The trapper looked at his newly blistered hands. Blood oozed from one and he wiped it on his pants.

"Yes."

"You will tell me?"

"I have no right," said Mike.

"You saved our lives. You have much right to say what is in your head."

"I don't want you to go," said Mike.

"You good man. My boys, they like you. I like you."

"I," said Mike softly. "No, I have no right."

"Please, I will listen to you."

"Before you came," said Mike, "I was lonely. I tried to live with my people but I didn't fit in, so I came back here to live alone. Until I met you and your boys, I didn't know life could be so good."

"Me, too. I have been happy here. You are kind, you no hit or yell. Fine, kind man."

"If I asked, would you and the boys stay?"

"Their father killed. I have no man. You take Indian woman and be such a man for us?"

"You would take me?" asked Mike eagerly. "An ugly man like me?"

"You no ugly, inside you most beautiful man I ever know."

"Then stay," said Mike.

Slowly he walked towards the dark haired woman and her white teeth flashed into a smile. Her arms opened and Mike Pardee walked straight into their grasp.

BOY ON THE DESERT

The hot sand burned the soles of the feet and made walking unbearable. Who would deliberately come to this godforsaken place? The bright light blinded the eyes, the sun burned down through the cloudless sky. The only thing that survived in this country either bit, or poked, or stabbed. It was nothing but a land of sand, rocks, leathery plants, rattlesnakes, scorpions, spiders, and lizards. Water was nearly nonexistent and more precious than gold. Without it, nothing could survive. In this country every man, plant, and animal needed it, and each fought for it in its own way, and without it died.

The wagon train that passed through on the way to California took the wrong fork in the road. It didn't take Apaches, renegades, or any man to bring down that group of twenty-seven people. The desert did that all by itself. The hot sun baked the creaking wagons during the day, and the cold at night under bright stars further sapped the strength of man and animal. When the water ran dry, and long before the wood of the barrels began to warp, the horses, the mules, and the oxen were dead. They lay sideways, drying up under their leathery skin with the harnesses of the wagons still strapped to them. The people lasted a few more days, and then their tongues dried out, turned black, and men, women, and children whistled out their last breaths through parched throats.

Little Willie drank the last from the canteen his parents held out for him, and then the five-year-old boy watched them slowly gasp out their last breaths. Hours later, when they did not move from the bed of the wagon, and after attempting to poke them awake, the boy cried and then did his best to climb down. From the back of the wagon he dropped the rest of the distance to the hard packed dirt of the ground. It was hot and the rays of the sun burned the boy's head and heated up the surface of his clothes and burned through them. It was painful and the boy sought shade under the wagon.

Through the rest of the day the boy lay there. All he heard and saw was the dry stillness of the New Mexico desert. There was no movement and the air and everything around him was made stifling hot by the rays of the fierce sun. The only sound he did hear were the buzzing flies, and they cared not on what object they settled and laid their eggs. Man or beast made no difference to their need for flesh and moisture.

Just as the sun was beginning to set and the intensity of the heat began to break into a delicious coolness, the boy heard the wail of an animal. It came from far-off and was a unique and thrilling cry. Others joined it. His father had called them something. The cries continued and then came closer. In between the long wails came yips and all types of high pitched calls. In fear, he fingered the small pocket knife he carried. He saw one of the creatures come running and behind it came others. It was a gray streak that blended with everything around it. It moved like a ghost and danced on four legs. It made no sound as it ran.

"Coyotes," said Willie out loud.

The boy remembered. They looked like dogs, but they were not. Father told him so. They were too skinny and fast for a dog. Their bodies were all slanted angles with pointed snouts and sharp teeth. These they bared at the boy. Growling, they came running in, and one animal began tearing at the flesh of a large ox. Then came brown flash after brown flash, faster than the boy could see. There was the sound of grinding and tearing, the gnashing of teeth, and deep throated growls. Both close and far away, was the repeated howling and wailing. More and more of the four-footed beasts responded to the call and came in to feast. These creatures, too, did not distinguish between man and animal, and they tore and ate hungrily on the dead flesh.

At first, fear of the toothy animals and their gruesome tearing of flesh frightened the boy. He lay under the wagon, and in his little fists he held a rifle that he gathered from one of the fallen victims. One large male coyote came running up to the boy and bared its teeth. Willie brandished the rifle before him and the coyote backed away with a snarl and went to feed on meat already dead. As big as the Winchester was in the boy's hands, he held it before him as he would a big stick and not as the weapon for which it was intended. Another time the always hungry pack would have stalked and killed the boy. But all this meat was just lying there, ready to be eaten. The coyotes ate and gorged themselves. When their stomachs were full, they simply lay down, curled up into furry balls, and went to sleep. They would stay and eat all of the meat, and would tear and gnaw even at the bones until they were cleaned white and tooth scarred.

The lad didn't know this. He watched in self-defense and listened to the crunching of teeth. How ferocious and aggressive they were at tearing and biting flesh, as if they were in a terrible hurry to satisfy a hunger that could never be satiated. They seemed to swallow large hunks of meat whole, and the youngster could see the slim bellies of the four-footed animals swell until they hung distended beneath them.

Eventually, it was too much for the boy and he tired. Despite the scene before him, his body betrayed him and he became thirsty and hungry. He dare not move from beneath the wagon. He lay there in misery knowing first-hand what death was and wondering numbly when it would come to him. Still, he held the rifle tightly in his hands, and only after a long struggle with himself, did he succumb to drowsiness and fall asleep. The night air turned cold and the boy shivered without waking.

It was the growling of animals and the crunching of bone that awoke him in the morning. As the rays of the sun fanned over the landscape, heat began to rise from the ground and with it the temperature of the air. Mixed with the rising heat was the nauseating stench of dead and rotten flesh. The boy watched the jaws of several coyotes tear into the guts of a bloated ox, and bits of red gore and flesh covered the toothsome snouts of the beasts. It was not just the bodies of animals that he watched the coyotes devour. He tried to avoid the scene of the beasts eating human bodies, but could not. They lay before his eyes and all around him. He could hear tearing of flesh above him and knew they were at his parents. The boy cried, but there was no moisture for tears.

The morning passed slowly, and once again the beasts became gorged and finally lay down. The gruesome noise of feeding stopped. The coyotes would digest their fill, and then later it would begin all over again. The heat increased as the sun rose higher, and the hairy creatures curled up, covering their blood-soaked snouts. The boy lay panting under the wagon bed and now his thirst outweighed his hunger. His tongue became dry and began to hurt in his mouth. His throat was dry, too, and it was becoming difficult to breathe. Soon he would be like his parents and the end would come. It wouldn't matter then what these creatures did.

It was in that moment Willie spotted something he had not seen before. Among several coyotes that were lying down, played a bunch of young pups. Willie counted. At first he saw four of them and then five. They played with each other, biting with their tiny jaws, and he could even hear tiny sounds of yipping and growling. The boy watched fascinated, and then the mother got up and the five pups followed her. Willie, still holding the heavy rifle, got to all fours and scooted out from under the wagon and stood up. Instantly, the heat of the sun shone down on his bare head. It burned hot on his scalp, on his skin, and even through his clothing. Dragging the rifle with both hands, the boy began following the mother and her pups. The mother coyote was walking due west and the pups were following, and twenty paces behind, so was Willie.

The boy had no idea what he was doing, but he could not stay beneath the wagon one moment longer. Everywhere it was hot and under the sun it was worse, but the young pups intrigued him. The pups, unlike the adults, were cute. They did not seem so dangerous. Willie would no longer stay with the dead; the smell was getting worse. He would follow the pups and their mother before he became too weak. Already it was so hard to breathe. He could not swallow and his tongue swelled in his mouth, dry and awful, and it hurt.

The mother coyote speeded up and so did the pups. Willie followed as best he could over the rough ground. At times he forced himself to run, still carrying the heavy gun. Finally he released the rifle and let it fall. Even without the load, the exertion made him pant. Willie began to panic. Still, the boy kept eye contact with the mother and pups and continued to follow. Several times the lad tripped and fell, but he got back up, determined not to give in.

This went on for a long time. Often the boy could not see the coyotes. The sun was bright and hot, and the fur of the animals blended with the landscape. Finally, the boy fell and he lay there to rest. When he made himself stand on his feet, he shaded his eyes and looked into the distance. As hard as he searched, he could no longer see the animals he was following. Yet, Willie struggled to continue. If the pups went in this direction, towards the setting sun, the boy would follow too.

As Willie staggered along, the sun slowly lowered until it shone directly in his eyes. Why did the mother lead her pups this way? Is this where they lived? Was there a cool hole in the ground? Did they drink water? They must drink water. All living creatures drink water. Instinctively, it was water that the boy thought about now and he continued to move forward, dragging himself along with the last of his strength. Again he fell, and this time he hurt his knees.

The sun lowered more and dropped down behind some high mountains leaving the purple shadows of twilight. With the absence of the sun, it began to get cooler. The boy sat up and looked at his torn pants and his bloody knees. His instant thought was that his mother would be very angry, and then he remembered, and again he cried. All his body could manage were dry gasps of breath and again there was no moisture for tears. As the boy sat, he finally raised his head and looked off in the distance. There he saw the glint of light on water and a wide ribbon of a river.

Willie rubbed his eyes and then made a great effort to stand. Once to his feet, he found new strength to continue. He shuffled down a steep incline and began to walk through tight brush that tore at his clothes. He did not know it, but he was in the floodplain of the great Pecos River. Each step was now descending and he walked under the shade of trees. There was the sound of rushing water. Pushing through more brush, he walked over green plants to the gravel bank. He fell off the bank into the fast flowing river nearly three feet deep. The boy struggled to stand up, but the water was over his head. He was now floating face down, his body spread horizontal in the stream.

Willie panicked and opened his mouth. Cold water rushed in. He swallowed and it hurt his dry throat. He needed air and he kicked with his feet and splashed with his hands. His head came up above the water for a second. The boy sucked in air and then he was surrounded by water again. He struggled against the current and flailed hands and feet. It did no good. He was floating and being pushed along with the swift current. Just when he could hold his breath no longer, his hands out before him, struck something solid. It was a large boulder. Willie reached with finger tips. The current pushed him, and his fingers slipped over and past the rock. Then, there were more boulders and rocks. A pile of gravel and sand formed by the current at a bend in the river made a shallow area, and the boy's body settled on it.

Willie struggled, managed to stand up, and found the current swirling around his hips. He gasped in a large amount of air and coughed water from his lungs. It made a thin spray from his mouth. Carefully, with cold liquid streaming from his clothes and hair, he walked towards the shore. There was no steep bank here and he stepped straight out of the river onto dry land. For the moment, his belly and chest was full of water and he continued to cough. Exhausted, he sat down in the dry gravel and sand. When he stopped coughing, he began to look before him. The water of the river was an astonishing blue, very clear and very clean. The boy was surprised to see such a large wide river, running magically through the middle of the desert.

As he thought about this, the sun sank further and finally set for the night. Looking up, Willie saw the final display of red and pinks before the light went out. Then it was dark. A coyote howled from behind and the lad shivered, not so much from cold for his body only felt cool and pleasant, but from the fear of being all alone. Despite the dark, the sky was clear and the boy was able to see the ground before him by the light of the many stars. Seeing a large dry stick lying in the sand, Willie grabbed it and stood up. He looked behind him and the shadows of small bushes and trees took on disturbing shapes. He stood there a long time before gathering the courage to move along, looking for some safe place to hide and spend the night.

He found it in a pile of boulders alongside the river. He nestled between several large rocks and lay down in dry sand. Surrounded by rock and wedged safely between boulders, he began to relax. Hunger pains gnawed at his insides, but he did his best to ignore them as he rested. Several times he got up, went to the river and lay down to drink, and then went back to his nest of safety. In this manner he spent the night.

Exposure to the heat and cold, lack of food and water, shock of his parents' death, the fear of the coyotes, the plunge into the cold river, and wet clothes, all contributed to the reason the boy lay in the sand between the rocks, shivering, and suffering from a sore throat. It was pre-dawn, the darkest hour of the night. The boy untangled himself from his position and stood up. The sun began to rise in the east and light formed around it. The light gently moved forward, then the orange disk exposed its round edges and more light spread across the land. Looking back towards the tree line, Willie could see a large round furry creature move among the bushes. When it moved, its glossy fur shook and shimmered. Surely this must be a very large bear. The boy watched and the animal disappeared into the brush. From far off came the now familiar high pitched wail of coyotes.

Willie shuddered at the thought of those creatures still feeding on the foul meat. Taking the little knife from his right pants pocket, the one his father had recently given him, he pulled out a sharp blade, picked up the stick he still had with him, and began to sharpen one end. It took all his strength to get the blade to slice off slivers of the hard, dried wood. Yet he worked on it and gradually a point began to form. It would take many hours of work to get it completely sharp. For the moment, the boy stopped, put his knife away, and then walked to the river. He lay down to drink. The cool water felt good going over his sore throat, and it felt even better in his empty belly.

Willie stood up and looked into the clear water of the river. He watched for fish, but saw none. Even if he had a way of catching one, how would he cook it? He wondered if he could eat one raw. He thought of going back to the wagons for string, hooks, matches, and even a pistol. The memory of the wild coyotes, the gruesome scene and his dead parents, again made him shiver. Despite his terrible hunger, he would stay near the river as long as he could. There was precious water here and the safety of the rock nest he had found. If a coyote came to try to eat him, he would get among the rocks and stab it with his stick. That was better than being in the open. Besides, water was even more important than food. The boy had discovered that. Living things die without water, thought Willie vaguely.

Stooping to pick up his stick, determined to carry it everywhere he went, Willie started for the tree line and the edge of the thick bushes. Food was on his mind. It was over there that the big bear was poking around. Willie came up to the huge bear tracks in the soft sand. The boy put both feet into one track. The back paw print was wider than his two feet together and twice as long. Following the tracks towards a bunch of bushes, he found little dark colored berries.

"Currants," said the boy out loud.

He was sure it was what his mother called them. He picked one and popped it in his mouth. It tasted tart and his lips puckered. His hunger driving him, he began to gather as many as he could into his little hands, and shoved them into his mouth as fast as he could, chewing and swallowing. This went on for a long time. There were a lot of berries, all of them ripe, some of them overripe. They would not last long. He must eat as many as he could. In a few more days they would be no good, or bears would come back and eat them all.

After a long time, Willie began to feel somewhat sick. He decided to stop eating, but how wonderful it was to have a full stomach. He could feel his tummy churning. Still, he must have more food or die. Willie decided to follow the bear tracks. They led beneath the huge cottonwood trees and to a rotten log. The log was torn up. The tracks continued and the boy followed. He came to more berries.

Willie got the idea to collect them on a large piece of bark from the old log.

Willie picked berries and filled the rounded piece of bark with them. This he carefully carried all the way back to his rock fort. There was a high place, a type of round ledge on the top of a boulder, and here the boy placed his food. After the morning forage, his belly now full, the boy decided to lie down and rest. Again he wedged himself between the walls of rock and fell into a deep sleep.

It was the howling of the coyotes that awoke him. They were not far off. Willie wondered if they had finished eating all the dead from the wagon train. As hungry and vicious as those animals seemed, Willie knew that they would come for him next. The youngster sat up, pulled out his knife, and began to sharpen his stick in earnest. He was determined to put a sharp point on it before he did anything else. All afternoon the boy worked, and slowly the tough wood splintered away to form the point. Satisfied, Willie put his knife away and stood up. He held the spear near the middle and practiced thrusting it. He was proud of his work.

The boy went back down to the river to drink. He would never be able to satisfy his need for water. Nor would he feel comfortable about leaving the stream. Again the thought of having to go back to the wagon train for items that he needed made him shiver in disgust. He was not even sure he could find his way back to the wagons. That pack of coyotes would surely kill and eat him, if they could. He would not let them—not as long as he had the spear. Not as long as he was alive and well.

Before night came, Willie gathered long dry grass that grew along the banks. This he carried back to his bed among the rocks and formed a soft nest. He picked lots of it, and made many trips. Tonight he would have enough of the soft material to lie on and to cover himself up. He thought of rain, and then forgot about it. In this country, rain did not come. Or at least he didn't think it did.

Willie lay down and went to sleep. He awoke to the many noises of the night. From time to time he heard splashes in the stream, always the yipping and howling of the coyotes, and one time he awoke and sat up to the sound of a terrible scream. It repeated itself. It sounded something like the high pitch scream of a woman, a terrifying sound, and then the boy identified it. He had heard it while on the wagon with his mother and father. It was a mountain lion. A cougar his father had called it, a wild cat.

The boy burrowed back down into his nest of dry grass. Before he could help himself, Willie began to cry. Thoughts of his parents would not leave him. He was alone and afraid. It would not be long before the coyotes would come to get him. His stomach reminded him that berries were not enough. He shook with convulsive sobs and felt the hot tears roll down his cheeks and off his face. He cried a very long time until he was exhausted, and only then did he fall asleep.

In the morning the boy got up, took his spear, and went down to the river to drink and wash.

"Cleanliness is next to godliness," Willie blurted out loud, repeating what his mother said everyday.

His mouth tasted yucky and pasty. Willie ran his tongue

over his teeth and they felt mossy. Following the ritual his parents taught him, he walked to a bush. He broke off a stick, and with his knife sliced one end over and over until it was a soft mass. This he placed in his mouth and rubbed and brushed his teeth with it. This was something his mother and father made him do; he saw no reason to stop now. Thoughts of his parents made him very sad. Willie looked out over the stream and across it to the limitless view of the flat desert and mountains beyond. If only his parents were here with him.

Hot tears again came into the boy's eyes, but this time he pushed them back. He would be strong. His parents told him to always be strong. Picking up his spear, Willie headed back for the line of currant bushes near the large cottonwood trees. Lost in thought, he walked along with his head down. Near the berry bushes he heard a soft grunt and the ground vibrated. Willie looked up. Not more than twenty feet away was a large bear looking straight at him. The bear opened its mouth and growled fiercely. Then it leaned back and stood up on its hind feet, its two front paws and arms tearing at the air. Willie stared at the long claws and the sharp teeth. The boy cringed in fear, thrusting the pointed end of his spear before him. The bear roared again.

"Don't you growl at me!" shouted the lad without thought.

The massive animal dropped to all fours. It rushed at the boy. There was suddenly a big explosion and a hole formed in one eye of the bear and red flowed. Willie watched the beast stop and fall flat under its own weight. The child turned around and fifty feet behind him, he saw a man dressed in buckskins holding a smoking rifle. Willie turned with his stick in his hand pointing it at the man.

"Well, sonny," said the bearded frontiersman. "Is that any way to thank me?"

*1st Printing, *THE SHOOTEST,* July/August 2007

Peach
Peach

DEATH COMES IN THE AFTERNOON

Sam Cook rose before dawn and washed his face in the pitcher and basin. He threw the water from off the front porch of his cabin and then took pieces of cut wood from the pile stacked against the wall and under the porch roof. These dry pieces he stuffed into the cast iron stove. Picking up a sliver of pitch pine, Sam lit it with a sulfur match and threw it down into the stove and watched it burn and catch onto the larger and dryer logs. As the fire began to build, Sam took down the cast iron frying pan and began breakfast.

First he cut up bacon into the pan, and as the fat melted and began to sizzle, he took from a basket three eggs he had gathered the night before. He cracked them over the spitting grease and was careful not to break the yokes as they slipped from their shells into the heavy pan. The aroma rose and mixed with the fragrance of the steaming pot of coffee. Sam hummed, *The old gray, mare, she ain't what she used to be*, and smiled. From the one window facing east, he watched the sunrise. It was going to be a beautiful clear day. There was not a cloud in the sky and

Sam saw the last star wink out with the spear of bright orange coming from the rising circle of the sun.

The lone rancher completed breakfast and tossed the fork, coffee cup, plate, and pan into a large bucket of water. He finished dressing, put on heavy boots, laced them tightly, and grabbed a homemade wooden fishing pole. Outside he picked up a can of worms and walked toward the stream that ran through the hundred and sixty acre homestead. As he approached, a small herd of cattle scampered away from the river and into a clump of cedars and piñon pines. Reaching the upper part of the stream, and the highest part of his land, Sam took a moment to look down on his cabin and across the spreading acres. Miles of open Colorado land glistened under the bright sun. Behind him, still in shadow, rose the thirteen thousand foot peaks of the Wet Mountains.

Sam was no slacker; he had worked hard at scything hay for the coming winter. He had tons of it stacked up in the bottomland along the river. This was a good year and his herd had already doubled. By spring, there should be another bunch of fine calves and he would have many steers to ship to market for his first cash crop. With the money, he would buy more female breeders and another bull. Perhaps he would add to his cabin, build on two more bedrooms, one for a future wife and another for any children that might come along. Sam Cook was proud of his homestead and hoped to file on another quarter section by hiring a helper and making an agreement to buy it outright once it was proved up.

Sam had a rule for Sundays, a pact he made with God.

As long as he was strong and able, he would never work on the Sabbath, but would spend it resting and reading from the Bible. It was the way his mother raised him.

And, what better way to greet the day then to fish in his own trout stream? The trout in the many holes that formed as the stream ran across his land were sleek and fat. There were so many of the silvery creatures, if he was careful, Sam would never fish them all out. Besides, their fine pink meat made a delicious afternoon meal, along with greens from his garden, and fresh coffee.

Sneaking up on the first good hole, Sam smiled as he dropped a baited hook into the stream. Instantly, he felt a tug—he pulled. A trout came flying out of the water, hooked soundly. The young rancher flipped it up and out onto the bank. The trout flopped noisily. Sam grasped the body of the fish in one hand, placed his other thumb in its mouth, and pulled back until the trout's spine was broken. He found a forked stick and slipped one end into a gill and slid the trout down to catch in the crotch of the fork. This was repeated as Sam fished his way down the stream. By late morning he had five fat trout and, with great contentment, he walked back to his one room cabin.

In many ways man is a creature of habit. On Sundays it was especially so for Sam Cook. He leisurely cleaned the trout, put them in a crock, and submerged it in a rock tank of running water that came from the stream. This was a system he had built with his own hands and it worked well to keep meat and other items cool. Next, he sat on a comfortable homemade chair and read from the Good Book. He stopped over the words: *Greater love hath no man than this, that a man lay down his life for his friends.*

After reading, Sam sat solemnly in the chair and looked out over the land—his land—land that the government, and a greater power, had let him file on. He loved this place and its beauty. From the porch he felt the rising heat of the sun and watched its rays reflect on the distant river. How precious water was to his ranch. Grass and hay could be irrigated and grown, cows and horses fed and watered, and the way of the rancher sustained.

Sam Cook took pleasure in these Sundays, sitting quietly alone on the porch. He laid his head back and rested his eyes and slept with the weight of the Bible on his lap. Sam slept in peace for a short while and then the nightmares came. They were always the same—men in blue against men in gray, thousands of them roaring in battle after battle—thunder and decimation, cannons booming—rifles blasting and bayonets flashing—men falling, screaming, praying, dying. The dream melted into reality—an explosion—flying off a precipice, plunging through the air and splatting heavily into water—agonizing pain to ribs and head. Floating powerless and drifting—strong hands pulling from the current—soldiers attending wounds, men in hospital beds, moaning and suffering.

Sam Cook awoke with a start and continued on with the thoughts the dream had provided. By the time his wounds had healed, the war had ended. He was one of the lucky ones. He had lost no eye, no arm or leg; he was whole, or at least outwardly so, and the scars of war he retained were only those of the mind. Taking his corporal's pay of four months, at thirteen dollars a month it totaled fifty-two dollars. Sam managed to "rescue" a mule, a LeMat pistol, rifle, ammunition, and a few days ration of food. Wearing his blue uniform, he started a long slow bareback ride west.

It was after many weeks of travel that he found this piece of Front Range land. Sam filed on it and it became his. Everything here he had made and formed with his own hands. Even the cows were mavericks he had captured and branded with his /C mark. Sam Cook was as content as he had ever been in his life. Finally, here was a chance to make something of himself. In the spring, he would sell his cash crop of beef, go east to find a ranch hand and, if he was very lucky, a wife.

After lunch of fried trout and fresh greens, Sam saddled his buckskin gelding, a horse he purchased from the sale of a few mavericks. He rode several miles to the nearest general store, which stood by itself along a new stagecoach spur. It served as grocery and supply store, post office, coach depot, bar, and restaurant to those ranchers and homesteaders coming in great numbers from the East. Behind it were a corral and a small stable. In time, this place may even grow and become a town.

Sam rode in and noted the brands on the horses tied to the front railing. There were Montoya's vaquero's and Garcia's, and there were also the brands of the newcomer, Jack Blakely. Blakely was a man of no known background who had come west, bought land, and then began to push others off their homesteads and steal their cattle. He would buy them out cheaply, or kill to get what he wanted. He now owned large sections of land, no one knew how many, or the number of steers he ran. Jack Blakely never traveled alone; he always had two gunmen by his side. He was a man with a big belly and big appetites. He pushed people around and folks, not fighters, just naturally backed up.

Sam dismounted and tied his reins to the crowded railing. Taking two gunnysacks, he went through the main doors and turned right into the store. From the bar he heard raucous laughter coming from men who had drinks behind their belts. Ignoring the noise, he entered the store with its mixed aromas of coffee, leather, licorice, peppermint, and other odors too numerous to identify.

"Hello, Bill!" called Sam with a smile.

The storeowner, Bill, stood behind a long counter; a grim look was on his face. He recognized Sam and then smiled.

"Hello, Sam. Good to see you."

The slim aproned owner bent down and came up with two white sacks filled with items, which he placed on the counter.

"Got your supplies all bundled up in these flour sacks. Everything including the ammunition for that crazy LeMat revolver you carry."

"Good, I only have five chambers loaded."

Sam took the itemized price list Bill handed him, glanced over it, and then paid the bill with coin. Bill leaned over and began to whisper. Sam's jaw tightened as he reached into the flour sack and took out .40 bullets, primers, patches, shot, and black powder. He loaded the remaining four chambers of the LeMat and its lower shotgun barrel. This took some time.

"Listen, Sam. Jack Blakely and his two hard-looking hombres came in this morning. They're next door and looking for you."

"Appreciate the advice, and the warning. But I won't be pushed by Jack Blakely."

"Sam, this is no time to take chances."

"Give me one of those sarsaparillas," said the rancher.

"They want your place," whispered Bill, "backed up against the mountains the way it is. That stream never dries up like those others do around here. You better go."

"A man who runs and hides is just postponing the inevitable," exclaimed Sam.

"But there are three of them!"

"Faced more than that in the war. If they come after me, I'll try to take it outside."

"They won't give you no fair fight," protested the merchant.

Bill let out a great sigh, shrugged his thin shoulders in hopelessness, and brought the drink Sam asked for. Sam popped the top off the cool sarsaparilla, took a swallow, and finished loading the revolver. He holstered the pistol and turned from the counter.

Into the store sauntered Jack Blakely followed by two bearded men. One man limped with his right foot, and another had a jagged scar that went along his lower jaw and disappeared down his neck and behind his neckerchief. The man with the scar wore two guns, the other had one in a holster and another shoved down in his front belt. Jack carried a holstered revolver around his thick belly.

"Well, well, well," said Jack Blakely. "The great Sam Cook has finally come to town. Hear tell you work six days a week and rest on Sunday."

"That's what they say," responded Sam easily.

"I been looking to speak to you."

"What about?"

"Your spread. I want it."

"I don't have clear title yet, but that's no matter. I'm not selling."

"That ain't friendly. You know I get what I want."

"So far you have. This time—No!"

"Folks told me you're a hard man. I brought Jake and Jesse with me to change your mind."

The two men with Jack suddenly laughed and the one with the scar spoke.

"We fought fer the south. We hear you're a Yank."

"Was. Rancher now."

"Now, that's funny," answered Jake. "Our boss here told us you either sell or we retire you."

"How's that?"

"With these," responded Jake, patting one of his pistols.

"What I figured," said Sam Cook. "I tell you, boys, if you draw those weapons, you're dead men."

Both Jake and Jesse stood silent, feet spread apart, their hands near their pistols.

"Haw!" brayed Jack Blakely loudly. "I heard tell you had grit. You sell or face my boys. Now what is it?"

"I told you, Jack—No Sale!"

"Okay then," Blakely stated grimly and jumped back. "It's your funeral!"

Jake, the man with the scar, drew first and fired. Sam reacted, his LeMat in hand, and shot back. Jake's bullet hit the rancher high up in the left shoulder. It jerked Sam back and sideways, making Jesse's first bullet miss him. Sam fired again and hit Jake in his breastbone and he fell back dead. Sam thumbed the hammer a second time and pulled the trigger. Blood splattered from Jesse's right leg. Jesse aimed and shot Sam in the chest. Sam, now on the floor, fired and the bullet struck Jesse in the forehead. The man was dead before he hit the wooden planks. Complete quiet replaced the blast of gunshots. The smell of gunpowder and its thick smoke hung in the air of the general store.

"Sam!" yelled Bill from down behind the counter. "Are you all right?"

There was no answer. With gun raised, Jack Blakely came from the side and stood over the prone figure of Sam Cook.

"I don't believe it," snarled Blakely. "This Union boy killed my best men."

"Is, is he dead?" stammered Bill.

"Looks like it. Now I get his ranch anyway."

"You're a hard man, Blakely," said Bill. "Sam Cook was a friend of mine."

"This here's a hard country. It's made for those who can take what they want."

"It's not right."

"Yeah? You better watch what you say, Bill. I can run you out, too, and take over the whole shebang!"

Sam Cook opened his eyes and managed to raise his revolver."

"Blakely," whispered Sam. "This time you don't win."

Jack turned, saw the aimed pistol, and managed to shout out one word, "No!" From the lower barrel, the shotgun fired. The discharge took Jack Blakely full in the face. The man fell forward. Bill leaped over the counter and ran to his friend.

"Sam, talk to me!"

The rancher's eyes flickered open and he looked up.

"Sam, I'm so sorry."

"Me, too," whispered the dying man. "See my ranch goes to some decent homesteaders—maybe one with a pretty woman."

Bill heard the long gentle sigh of air escaping from Sam Cook's lungs and he knew his friend was dead.

*1st Printing, *THE SHOOTEST,* November/December 2007

KID ON THE RUN

The Mississippi River ran along the edge of the busy city of St. Louis in a wide sweeping arc. It swept under and past the long rows of docks and the hundreds of steamers and packets that lined its banks. The War Between the States had just ended. It was a cold November and a shivering eleven-year-old lad looked on at the men who labored to unload boxes and bales of supplies from the steamers into waiting wagons. The boy was poorly dressed and the clothes he wore were dirty, ragged, and torn.

Otis Sutter stood and stared at the crates of molasses and can goods. He could smell the sweet syrup. He had just filled his stomach with water from a pump and he could feel it slosh as he walked away from the river. It had been days since he had eaten properly and his empty stomach twinged in pain. The chilling cold seemed to go right through him and some of it settled in his bones. He was beginning a cough and a fever. He was dizzy and light-headed as he walked back to the little wooden fort he had made in the alley between two warehouses. It wasn't more than a wooden box that he had hammered together with used nails, a shelter he had been living in for months and his only home. His precious few possessions were hidden there in a hole that he had dug under the fort and covered with a loose board. In it were two blankets, an iron skillet, a broken knife, a fork, a large piece of metal in which he burned wood to keep warm at night, a box of matches, a hatchet with a broken handle, and bits of rags and cloth he used to stuff in the cracks to keep out the cold.

As Otis came down the alley he saw two angry men tearing away at his home. They turned and spied the boy and began to yell.

"Are you the one who made this here mess? Get on with you, boy. This is private property! We don't allow no bums!"

Otis stared in silence as the men wrecked the only shelter he had. He saw one of the men pick up the axe with the broken handle and began to smash the wooden boards apart. They broke the makeshift building into pieces and dragged the broken boards out of the alley and tossed them into a wagon. Everything the boy owned was now lost—even the blankets and rags. The iron he burned wood in and the broken axe went into the back of the wagon.

"Get out of here, boy! We don't need no beggars living and stealing around here!"

The two men finished loading the debris into the wagon and then suddenly ran at the boy. Otis began a stumbling run. He managed to get some distance when he heard the men laugh. The boy turned and watched them walk to the wagon, get aboard, and drive off into an opening in one of the warehouse doors. Otis stood and stared and then slowly walked away. The wind was starting to blow and with it came spits of snow and it was getting colder. The lad pulled up the collar on his coat in an effort to get warm but it did not help. He was without a heavy coat and gloves, and his hands, ears, and top of his head were cold. If he didn't find shelter soon he was going to be in trouble.

The boy trudged along moving as quickly as he could to try to warm himself, but he was weak and the best he could manage was a slow shuffle. He came to a general store that was in the poorer neighborhood near the docks. The boy walked up wooden steps and opened the door with a frosted windowpane and stepped inside. Immediately he smelled coffee, peppermint, leather, oils, perfumes, and a myriad of other goods that commingled and remained in the air. It was delicious to the boy and his stomach rumbled. He felt dizzy relief inside the warmth of the store and naturally gravitated towards the large round potbellied stove in the middle of the room. The boy put out his dirty hands to feel the heat of it and then he heard the voice.

"You, boy! You dirty beggar! Get out! I told you to never come in here. Now out with you or I'll thrash your hide!"

A little man with wire spectacles raised a broom above his head, came from behind the counter, and rushed at the boy. Reluctantly, Otis turned from the threat of the storekeeper and headed for the door. This he opened before the little man reached him and he closed it on the angry owner of the store. Instantly, the cold wind blew through the boy's thin clothing and he cringed and longed for the warmth he had left behind. The boy ducked his head and slowly made his way down the wooden steps, the wind pushing hard against all of his body. Otis made his way to the dirt road and then turned his back to the wind and walked with it towards the city.

Otis was so cold, tired, dizzy, and weak he could hardly think. His toes in his father's large boots were freezing, so were his fingers, his ears, and his nose—his entire body shivered. This time the boy did not have the strength to go on and he felt that soon he would fall and lay to freeze along the road. No one wanted to help an orphan and no one in this large city had ever shown kindness to him or come to his aid. He had found some odd jobs from time to time. But as he became weaker, dirtier, and hungrier, wearing the same smelly clothes with no soap to clean them, no one would hire him. The boy walked on slowly, putting one foot in front of the other, with no thought of where he was going or what he was going to do. It was an effort to move now, and he was becoming numb all over with the cold and he felt so weak, so very weak.

* * *

Alfred Spire took the pint bottle from his inner coat pocket, pulled the cork, lifted it to his lips, and tilted back his head and hand to swallow the amber liquid. It burned all the way down his throat and entered his stomach where it instantly warmed and soothed the old man. He staggered along now, heading back to his little shack down the alley and behind the saloons, stores, and warehouses that lay in the poor section by the river. It was getting dark and the wind was really blowing cold now and snow was collecting where it fell on the ground. It was going to be a bad winter storm and Alfred was thinking of his drafty little cabin with its warm potbellied stove and blanketed bed. The old man pulled up his coat collar against the cold and the heavy buffalo coat lapels felt good against his freezing ears. Alfred hurried now and bent his head to walk with the cold wind that blew at his back. Then he tripped over something lying in the dark of the alley and he swore.

Bending and turning around, Alfred peered drunkenly down at the dark object lying in his path. The old man swayed back and forth trying to focus his eyes in the dim light. *What's this? A bundle of rags? No. It looks like a body! Has somebody been stabbed or robbed and the body placed here to be out of the way? It won't be the first time.*

The old man didn't want to get involved. He turned away; but as he did so, he heard a low groan. It was not the voice of an adult; it was the voice of a young person. Again the old man turned and this time he reluctantly bent down on one knee and felt at the ragged body.

"Mom," a faint voice drifted through the cold wind. "Mom, I'm so cold."

The old man recognized the voice of a boy. He felt the bundle before him with both hands. One hand found the upper body, and then traveled up to the head. The man's hand touched the boy's forehead in the dark and it was on fire.

"This here's a very sick youngster, but how did he come here?"

The drunken man's head cleared a bit in the rushing cold wind and deciding, he put both arms under the bulk of the body on the ground and lifted. There was nothing to the lad; he was light as rags. Gaining his balance, the old man creaked to a standing position, turned, and swayed with the bundle in his hand and walked to his shack.

The air was suddenly filled with white swirls of snow, blowing sideways in the swift cold wind. The old man couldn't see more than a few feet in front of him. He looked to the ground, now covered in white, and tried to follow the open path of the alley. Coming to the end of the alley and up against the back of a building, the man swayed and turned left, carrying the small body that was becoming heavier now. He made his way along the side of the building, and there came to an opening and then his little shack. Alfred struggled to the door and fumbled with the bundle still in both hands. He managed to lift the latch and the wind pushed the door open wide and it banged against something. The old man entered, staggered to a cot-like bed and, as gently as he could, let the bundle of rags down onto it. Then he rushed to the door and, pushing against the wind, managed to close and latch it. Picking up a board that leaned against the wall, he barricaded the door.

Alfred turned and swayed. His head was clearing and becoming more sober with each moment due to the cold fresh air. Inside the cabin it was only degrees warmer than outside. Cold air rushed in everywhere through the cracks in the old shack and it made swishing noises as the wind blew. Alfred shivered, went to a small table in the middle of the room, found matches, and struck one. He lifted the glass of a lantern, lit the wick, lowered the glass, and adjusted the knob. Instantly the light grew and lit up the entire room. Next, the old man went to the cold potbellied stove and opened its lower heavy iron door. He looked inside. Alfred grabbed a shovel and box and began to clean out the cold ashes that had collected there. He closed the lower door and opened the heavier one above where he threw crumpled up paper and pine slivers. Lighting another piece of paper with a match, he let it drop. The pine slivers caught along with the paper and larger pieces of wood were added. Soon the fire in the old stove was roaring and the man added two large logs. Heat rose from the stove and began to warm the room. Alfred rubbed his cold hands above the stove, frowned, and turned to look at the bundle lying on his bed.

The man, feeling the last of his drunken glow fade, felt himself becoming cold sober. Looking across at the bed, for the first time he considered the seriousness of what he had done.

"Should I have minded my own business?"

His head hurting, he looked down at the young boy. The child was dirty, his clothes ragged and torn. Alfred surmised that some strange tragedy had struck the boy and he had come to this condition. The old man stared down at the sick and fevered lad and his heart went out to him. He felt a sudden conviction to do all he could for the youngster.

The man felt the boy's forehead. It was red and hot and dry, and the lad was mumbling in his delirium. Alfred took a cracked pitcher from the dresser and poured water into a pan. This he placed on the flat surface of the stove. Then he took a coffee pot, found beans, ground them and put the fresh grounds into the pot to make coffee. He added water and placed it to boil next to the other pan.

The old man looked at the boy again. The youth continued to mumble. He appeared to be eleven or twelve or somewhere in that age—the man couldn't tell. The youth was thin, so very thin. The child's face was tight against the bones of his skull. Alfred felt the boy's arms and legs beneath his clothing and they were all skin and bones. He began to undo the boy's coat and it tore at the sleeves. Alfred hesitated and then returned to his labor. He removed his coat, the two shirts the boy was wearing, his coarse oversized boots, and his dirty socks and pants. The youngster lay in filthy underwear. Alfred quickly covered him with blankets and a heavy buffalo robe. The boy stopped shivering and seemed to rest more comfortably under the heat of the blankets and from the rising warmth of the cabin.

When the water came to a boil, the man poured the hot water into a basin. He added some cooler water from a bucket and then felt it. He took a clean rag and bar of soap and went to the boy and washed him. At least the lad smelled and looked cleaner. Alfred hoped the water on his hot skin would bring down the fever. His face already looked less red. The man put aside the dirty water and went to the stove. He poured a cup of coffee for himself and one for the child.

Alfred hesitated and then added some of his whiskey to the boy's tin cup. He went over, raised the lad's head, put the cup to the lips of the young man, and tried to get him to drink. Much of the liquid flowed down the chin of the feverish child onto the bedding, but from time to time the youngster swallowed and coughed. For the first time, Alfred smiled. He put the boy's cup on the table, sat down and relaxed next to the warm stove. He turned the chair so he could see the youth's face. While he watched him breathe, he sipped his coffee. The old man gradually tilted his head and fell asleep in the warmth of the cabin.

Sometime during the early morning hours the shouting of the feverish boy awakened the old man. Confused at first, Alfred did not know who was in the cabin with him. His mind cleared and he rushed to the bedside. Alfred had a terrible headache. It had been a long time since his whiskey soaked brain and body had gone without alcohol. The first thing the man did was pull out his pint bottle to take a swig. Halfway to his mouth he stopped. He looked down at the sick lad and reluctantly popped on the cork and put the bottle away.

For the next few days the youngster lay close to death. He was so sick and weak; his starved and emaciated body did little to fight the fever. The old man could not afford to bring a doctor, even if he could find one who would come to that area of town. Alfred was the child's sole caretaker. He cared for the boy day and night and not once in the following days did he take a drink. For the first time in ten years, Alfred Spire had someone else to think of other than himself. A boy's life was at stake, an innocent child, one who was far more important than his worthless self—so, even though Alfred battled with his own delirium tremors, he remembered the boy and left the whiskey corked.

During his high fever the lad talked mostly to his mother.

"Mom, where are you? I am so sick, Mother. Help me! Please help me."

Alfred put a cool cloth to the child's head and rubbed alcohol on his chest to cool his fever.

"Thank you, Mother. Thank you. That feels better."

At times the boy even reached out and grasped the hand of the old man. As the congestion worsened and the lad's lungs filled with fluid, the youngster continued his delirium and talked and cried out in a rasping, choking voice.

"Father, no, no—Indians—they are taking the hides. No, God, no—don't die, Father. Let them take the hides. We can shoot more buffalo. Don't die, Father! Don't die!"

The boy would shake and scream. Alfred held the feverish child until his trembling stopped, his own eyes filled with tears. Piece by piece, scream by scream, Alfred put together the young boy's tragic life. It was when the child called to his mother that the old man broke down.

"Mother, don't go. I can work hard and scrub the floors. He can pay me your wages. You look so sick, mother. Please, don't go."

As painful as this was to Alfred, his heart broke when he heard these words repeated over and over.

"No! She's not dead—she's not dead! Don't put her in that box. Stop! Don't bury her. She's not dead. Mama, talk to them. Tell them they are wrong."

Hour by hour the story came out. Sometimes it was through screaming in the middle of the night—sometimes in rasping sobs as Alfred wiped down the boy's hot forehead. He yelled at men who came and took his home and everything his parent's owned.

"You can't take the horse, too. My father owned her square—he didn't owe the mercantile that much. I ain't going to no orphanage—I'm not an orphan. I got kinfolk in St. Louis. Let me go. Let me go. I said, I ain't no orphan."

The old man listened to the boy's story and it tore his heart out. Alfred vowed to save the lad's life if he could, to never take another drink if the lad did survive, and to become his caretaker and friend. The old man worked hard over the youngster and only slept in small fits as he did everything to fight the child's fever. Over and over again Alfred rubbed the boy down with alcohol, the very same store of it that he had put aside for his own drunken needs. Now he was putting it to good use, a far better use than he ever imagined. Alfred kept the temperature in the drafty cabin warm by constantly filling the stove with wood. Still, none of this seemed to be doing any good. The lad was failing fast.

Alfred recalled Indian remedies he had learned when he lived with the Cheyenne. He made a sweat bath by building a tent of robes around the bed and then heating and laying hot rocks on the floor under it. By pouring water over them, billows of steam rose up. He did this over and over again. The steam and intense heat entered the boy's lungs and cleared the congestion enabling him to breathe again. Alfred went out and purchased a chicken. This he cut up and made into a herbal broth. The boy would not eat so Alfred held the lad's nose. When he opened his mouth, the man put in spoonfuls of the nutritious liquid. Time and again the boy coughed it up, or it went into the bedding, but with great patience the old man got some of the broth down into the boy's stomach.

Early in the morning of the sixth day, the lad opened his eyes and had his first lucid moment. There, standing before the boy, was the newly washed face, groomed beard, and combed hair of the now sober Alfred Spire. The old man stared down at the youth and smiled.

"There you are, lad. Would you be wanting something to drink or eat?"

"Where am I?" asked the boy.

"Don't worry, you be safe in the cabin of Alfred Spire. I be your friend, boy. You were sick, and now you are better. Please take some of this good soup, lad. It will make you feel good. You have been a long time without it."

The boy was too hungry to refuse and greedily he swallowed spoonful after spoonful of the nutritious soup. He drank half a cup of coffee and fell into a deep and restful sleep. After that, he began to recover and his coughing and congestion became less. In two weeks he gained weight and looked snug and fit in the store-bought clothes Alfred had purchased for him. In that time there was much occasion for the two to talk. The old man told Otis Sutter of how he came to know his life story. Then the old man shared his own.

"Boy," said Alfred as he and Otis walked along the docks, watching the stevedores loading and unloading the packets. "I know what you been through—losing your folks and all. You see, lad. Long ago I walked jist about the same path you be walking now. I, too, was an orphan—a bit older than you be—fourteen it was. I lived with my ma and pa on a little ranch out on the Great Plains. We didn't have much but we worked hard and were pretty happy—that is until that morning a band of renegades attacked. My ma, she died first—but, my pa, he tried to save me. He told me to run; hide in a deep arroyo. Then, he took the only horse left in the corral and jumped on him bareback—he rode past the renegades and they follered after him. They ran him down and shot him—then they burned the ranch after taking what little we had that interested em."

Alfred cleared his throat and brushed his eyes with his sleeve. He looked at the boy and saw he was crying too.

"I hid in that arroyo all day and that next night—morning came and a Cheyenne hunting party rode by. They often watered their horses at our well. Pa always let them be and my ma, well, she always seemed to find a pan of sweet cornbread that she left out on the fence post when she seen them coming. Them Cheyenne, they saw the smoke—and they came looking to see what happened. It was Broken Limb who saw my tracks and found me. He took me to his lodge and I lived with his family. It was there I came to know the western lands and the way of the Indian."

Alfred was silent for several minutes. He hung his head, looked down at the dock beneath his feet and spoke slowly. His voice was low and sad.

"I did a horrible thing—and I can't never forget. Something that was betrayal to my Cheyenne family. I began to slaughter buffalo, not to feed the tribe, but for sale. I left my friends and hunted for hide traders. I grew rich at it. Finally, sickened by the killing, I sold out. I had hid away my money, and slowly slipped into drinking. Did that for nigh ten years."

The old man put his arm around the boy's shoulders and looked down into his large sad eyes.

"Lad, it was not until I stumbled over you that night, cold, sick, and laying in the alley, that I had reason to think of someone other than myself."

Otis reached out and took Alfred's hand. He placed his small hand flat against the older man's larger gnarled one.

A few months later, Otis Sutter and Alfred Spire mounted saddled mustangs and rode across the prairie away from St. Louis. Behind them, each had a pack horse loaded with supplies. Both were heavily armed and dressed in new buckskins. They headed for the spires of the Great Rockies and the Colorado mountains.

"Ahh, this is the way to live, lad," exclaimed Alfred. "In open country."

"Pa and I often talked of going further west. Even Ma wished for our own land."

"I am sure your folks were good people, Otis."

"Alfred, I want to thank you for this—for all that you have done for me. If it wasn't for you, I wouldn't be here. When I was alone, I often longed to join my folks."

"And now, lad?"

"With you, life is good again."

"For me, too, Otis. Now cheer up. I've got to teach you to be a frontiersman—even if it kills you."

"I guess you got a right. After all, you already saved my life once."

Together, the old man and the boy laughed. Dust rose up behind the horses of the two travelers. A stranger from a boat on the river watched their slow passage as they disappeared into the distance.

*1st Printing, *THE LAKESHORE GUARDIAN,* June/August 2006

THE LAD FROM NORWAY

He was a great big wall of a man. All muscle and sinew built on a foundation of big feet and bones. He rose to a height of six foot four, topped with white blond hair, carrying a deep tan on fair skin, examining the world through pale blue eyes above protruding cheek bones. Upon initial encounter every man, woman, and child hesitated and came to a dead stop to look at this remarkable example of humanity.

How this exemplary product of Norse heritage came to the west is a complicated story. It began with a voyage on his father's fishing vessel and ended in shipwreck on the rocks off the coast of Maine. There the battered carcass of the twelve year old was succored by an old man who taught him the rudiments of English. When Sten Ogdahl's bones were healed, he set out upon a journey that led to the factories and slums of New York City.

After three years he tired of the slums and low wages, and fled the city to lay track for the railroads. The grueling drudgery of laying ties and steel in the isolated west, led him to the promise of good pay in the coal camps at Walsenburg, Colorado. There, Sten, like so many of his fellow immigrants, became indebted to the company store. He watched his fellow miners starve and die in the wretched mines. Above ground, families succumbed to disease and hunger in the slum camps. The armed guards under orders from the rich Industrialist Carnegie, kept the poor European Immigrants enslaved within the coal camps.

On a Saturday evening the Norwegian emerged black and dirty from the dark cave of a coal mine. He was really too big for the confines of the shafts and tunnels and often worked an entire shift stooped over, swinging a pick axe at an odd angle. Sten's anger grew with his indebtedness. The promise of good pay and working conditions was nothing but lies. The company stores charged high prices for everything they sold, forcing the workers into debt that would never be paid off. It insured virtual slavery. Few escaped, and if they did, a warrant for their arrest would follow.

"You not be keeping me here any longer!" announced Sten to one of the armed men.

"You don't leave until you pay off the company store!" ordered the man.

Sten clenched his right fist and circled his heavy arm to come in contact with the top of the guard's head. Down went the man into deep blackness. Sten picked up the unconscious guard's rifle and ran, dodging bullets from other Winchesters. He fired back and, for the first time ever, the company men ducked their heads in fear for their own lives.

* * *

I first met the big Norwegian when he came off the plains. He was covered with black coal dust, on foot, thirsty, and carrying his rifle as if it was a toy in his huge hands.

"Could I have a drink, sir?" he asked, standing at the water trough.

I had never been called sir in my life. When I nodded my head, he bent to drink from the horse trough.

"No!" I yelled in consternation and ran to pump the handle so he could drink the fresh water flowing from the spout. "Why man, don't you know you don't drink direct from an animal trough?"

He looked down at me with those pale blue eyes of his, a virtual mountain of a man. I was an old rancher, all alone on a quarter section. I never saw such a fine example of a grown man in all my life.

"I not be from this country," he said.

"Where you from?" I asked.

He stood up from drinking and I stopped pumping to listen. His face took on a vacant faraway stare, as if remembering.

"I come from a land of fiords, the deep sea caught between cliffs, topped by clouds and mountains."

For a man who did not speak English well, he had a way with words.

"Where's that place, stranger?" I asked.

"A land I be afraid I never see again, Norway."

I took a look at all that humanity. Already I was putting

those huge arms to work. He looked to be worth ten ranch hands in one.

"A man on foot out here is a rare thing," I commented.

"I like to walk."

"Are you looking for work?"

Again came that faraway look.

"I do, but treat me fair. I not be letting any man do me harm."

"Stranger," I said in alarm. "I never cheated no man. There's work to be done, but I have little I can pay."

"What work? What pay?"

"I give you room and board. Don't have cash."

"I work for no man for free. What be room and board?"

"I feed you and you sleep in the cabin for free."

"Not enough."

"Well," I said thinking on it, not wanting to lose this mountain of muscle. "Suppose you work one month. Do good and I'll give you a horse. It'll have to be a big one. See that black in the corral there? She's seventeen hands, part mustang, and part draft. I'll throw in a saddle."

"I work hard," answered Sten. "Do two men's work. Need pay."

"Tarnation, stranger! I'll sell a couple steers and pay you what they bring."

"How much?'

"Twenty dollars."

"Done," said Sten holding out his big right paw. "You shake hands with Sten Ogdahl. What be your name?"

I hesitated, looking at that huge mitt. Not wanting to offend him, I put out my arthritic hand. Just like I thought, he squeezed down hard and I jumped up and down and shouted.

"Let go, stranger! Let go! Don't squeeze it off!"

He let go, grinning ear to ear and showing snow white teeth.

"Name?" he asked again.

"Darrell Arnold," I told him. "I homesteaded this one hundred sixty acres and that there water hole behind the cabin, and part of that crick that runs through. Sometimes the crick dries up, but never the spring. I cut the hay along the stream and around the water hole. Place won't tolerate more than ten steers and ten horses. Got another forty head that run on open range, if the Indians and rustlers haven't taken em. I'm nigh on sixty, and it's too much for one old man."

"Where's family?" Sten asked.

"Never had no wife. My partner got kilt. Found him a few years ago in back of the ranch, up against Greenhorn Mountain. Couldn't tell if it was accident or deliberate. Been caring for this place by myself ever since. Was a time we ran five hundred head of steers on open range."

"Sten help you," he answered smiling again from ear to ear. "Good worker, you see."

He stooped down again and I started pumping. He appeared to drink a cow's worth of the wet stuff.

* * *

The Norwegian kept his word and worked until the clothes he wore started falling off him. First he braced and repaired the roof of the barn. He had a way of working with his hands, and he honed down tough cedar into usable pieces of wood. Then he cut all the existing hay with a scythe and piled it into the loft and on the barn floor. He cut straight cedars for posts and repaired the leaning corrals and fences. Next he mended the leaking roof of the cabin and straightened the sagging porch. He even made a new kitchen table and a cedar bed for himself.

He was a working fool, never standing idle from sunup to sunset.

I never heard him complain, and he seemed to enjoy using his vast physical strength. Halfway through the month I gave him the horse. He called the large mare Gertrude. A big horse for a big man. Before long a strange affection grew between that man and horse. He would pet her and talk to her and feed her scraps from the vegetable garden I had planted. It was remarkable how quickly he learned to ride and become one with the mare. He even got more speed out of her than I thought possible.

After the first month we went to town and I sold two steers and gave him twenty dollars. Sten wouldn't buy new clothes for himself but instead purchased apples and carrots for that fool horse of his. Soon she was a pet. She learned to open the corral gate and follow him around like a puppy dog. Gertrude sniffed at his pockets and pushed him from behind as he worked. That man had the patience of Job and would affectionately pet her head and then take her back to the corral. Not once did he ever lose his temper.

The months went by and in the fall I purchased clothes from the general store for the raggedy man. Nothing fit him and I had to take them back. The owner's wife took his measurements and from two of everything made pants, underwear, and shirts. Boots and a western hat had to be special ordered from a catalogue.

I never saw a man learn so much as quickly as Sten. Almost everything I taught him he caught on the first time. He learned to ride, push cattle, fix barbed wire, tend horses, track, shoot, and hunt elk and deer like a natural born cowboy. But, he never seemed to catch on to roping. And, he wasn't much with the old six-gun I bought him either, but he was dang good with a long gun. By the end of six months my new ranch hand was as formidable a westerner as I ever saw. He even developed my drawl with a faint hint of his native tongue.

Just before winter I counted the range cattle and returned to the ranch.

"Sten, have you seen any strange tracks on your daily rides?"

"A while back I saw some shod hoof prints up against the mountain. Why?"

"We're missing about twenty head of cattle. Half the herd."

"Which direction?"

"Towards Colorado City," I answered.

"Don't the buyers check the brand?"

"Some do. Suspect they slipped around town and up to Pueblo."

"Can we get em back?" Sten asked.

"Not enough of us, and if we leave, we might be cleaned out."

"You taught me to track, Darrell. I'll take Gertrude and

try to run them down."

I looked at him, amazed at his gumption and the speed in which he learned how to western.

"I counted three horses leading northwest," I said. "You'll pick up the tracks near the big rock next to the back canyon."

Sten gathered the Winchester and extra ammunition. I packed jerky and airtights in a saddlebag, along with a frying pan and spoon. Walking out to bridle and saddle his horse, Sten was every bit the cowboy. The pistol and big western hat looked small on his massive frame. I filled a canteen and hung its strap over his saddle horn.

"Sten," I spoke softly. "You take care. I'd rather have you safe, than get the cattle back."

"Darrell, I got to try."

"I know, son," using that word for the first time in my life. "You just be sure you get back here in one piece, you hear?"

Those blue eyes searched my face, and then the big man smiled.

"Okay, Pops," he said and dug his spurless heels into the mare.

The horse trotted off, leaving a cloud of dust to drift over me. I went in and got a loaded Winchester and sat down on the porch in a chair Sten made for me. I watched him fade out between the many piñon and cedar trees. The horse and rider turned into a tiny speck that disappeared into yellow grassland that rolled away for a hundred miles.

I didn't sleep much. I moved out of the cabin and lay in a bedroll in the brush. To be ready to move, I kept a horse saddled day and night, picketed with the bit out, so it could graze. I guarded the cattle and cabin, moving to a new lookout each morning. There was jerky, airtight beans, and water from a canteen. I lit no fire, and stayed hidden. No outrider was going to take me by surprise.

Constantly, I worried about Sten. That boy had come to mean more to me than my own ranch.

* * *

The herd's hoofprints were interspersed with those of the three shod horses. Sten dismounted and examined each print. Within a few miles he had the variations memorized. Now he would be able to identify the rustlers by their tracks. He speeded up and followed the trail at a gallop. Eventually he slowed down and began alternating between a fast trot and a lope. The horse continued on with amazing stamina. The sky faded from dusk to dark. The stars came out one by one and lit up the trail.

The rustlers built a cooking fire and the glow of it, despite cover, was seen from a great distance. Sten dismounted and tied the reins to the saddle horn. As he moved stealthily through the brush, Gertrude followed behind. They came up to the cattle that were settled down for the night. Some lowed softly in the stillness. The cook fire was out, but the woodsmoke hung in the clear dry air. Under the stars and the rising moon, light increased. Two men in bedrolls were easily seen. Somewhere the third man was standing guard.

Sten raised his hand and stroked Gertrude's forehead gently.

"Stay here, baby," he whispered.

He walked between stunted piñons and got as near to the sleeping figures as he dared. The moon was rising and with the added light there began to be shadows. Any one of them could be the guard. Sten stooped behind a pine and waited, Winchester in hand. The cattle continued to low, insects chirped, and an owl hooted. Occasionally, from far off, a coyote's high pitched howl echoed across the land. Sten waited.

It was the glow of a cigarette that gave the rustler away. The smell of smoke wafted through the air. Sten cautiously made his way towards the guard. Gertrude, thinking this a game, came quietly through the grass and pine trees. The guard heard the heavy step of the horse. He turned to see the animal push a man carrying a rifle into an open clearing. The startled guard drew his pistol and fired. A bullet hit the man somewhere in his upper body. The force of it threw him back and to the ground.

The cattle, startled by the gunshot, rose to their feet, bellowing frantically. A group of steers stampeded over one of the rustlers as he lay tangled in his bedding. The other outlaw jumped up, pistol in hand. He ran from the rushing herd and tried to identify who had blasted a gun and at what.

"To your left, Sam!" shouted the outlaw who had fired. "I shot at a feller!"

"Who is it, Bill?" called Sam.

"Don't know. All I saw was a big horse shoving a man into the clearing near the camp," answered Bill.

"Maybe you're seeing things."

"Go to blazes, Sam. What I saw was real. What's more I think I hit him."

Sam walked forward and stumbled over the third outlaw. The crushed body was in deep shadow. Sam stooped down and felt with one hand. His fingers came up with wet gore.

"Bill!" called Sam. "Charlie's dead. The herd stomped him bad."

"That's awful, Sam. But there's nothing we can do about it. Hush, now! We got to find that hombre."

Gertrude stepped out into the open. She leaned down and snuffled at the prone body of her master. She smelled blood and neighed.

"See that!" shouted Bill. "Now who's seeing things?"

Cautiously, both outlaws moved forward, pistols cocked and ready to fire. Gertrude snorted. She lowered her huge head and neck. Behind the cover of the horse, Sten came to his feet, rifle in hand. Aiming at both outlaws who were coming towards him, he held his fire. He did not want Gertrude to be hit. Grabbing the bridle, he guided the horse behind a large pine tree and tied the reins tightly to a branch. He ran in a circle to come up behind the outlaws.

"Drop your pistols," ordered Sten.

In unison the two rustlers turned and fired. Sten was kneeling behind a low piñon and the bullets went over his head. He fired back and hit one outlaw in the chest. The second man fired his pistol again and this bullet struck Sten in the side. He twisted and fell back. The outlaw continued to fire into the tree. Sten rolled to his right and shot the rifle one handed. The bullet struck the remaining outlaw in the head.

Sten lay back, beginning to feel the pain of the bullets in his right shoulder and his left side. He took a handkerchief and stuffed it under his shirt to try to stop the bleeding. There came the sounds of crackling branches, a loud neigh, followed by hoof beats. A soft dry muzzle rubbed against his face.

"It's alright, Gertrude." Sten spoke gently to his horse. "I'm just nicked some. It's okay, girl. Now stand still and I'll climb up."

Using the stirrups, Sten pulled himself up to his knees and then stood to lean against the saddle. Placing his left foot into the stirrup and a hand on the pommel, he hoisted himself up. Leaving rifle, outlaws, and cattle behind, he let Gertrude guide him towards the ranch. It took all his strength to hold onto the pommel. Eventually he passed out and fell to the ground.

* * *

From my cover I watched as that big pet horse of Sten's galloped up to the cabin. She neighed shrilly. I lunged for my horse, tightened the cinch, inserted the bit, and mounted. At the cabin I grabbed Gertrude's bridle. She was frantic and rolled her eyes. I saw blood on the saddle and let loose of her.

"Go!" I shouted to the horse.

She circled and took off at a gallop. I followed, trying hard to keep up. I found Sten's body lying in the soft sand of a deep arroyo. It was one of the few places where the ground was not hard clay. Sten was covered with blood. I dismounted and examined the wound in his shoulder and the one in his side. The side wound was already crusted over and the bleeding stopped. A bullet had merely made a deep crease in the soft flesh. Painful, but not serious. The bullet in the shoulder was a different matter. It was lodged just above his heart. I had to get it out and stop the bleeding or he would die. There wasn't much time left. He had already lost too much blood.

I built a small fire and held the blades of my knife and Sten's in the flames. With one, I probed for the bullet. It was deep and hard to reach. The bleeding increased. Using both knives, I located the piece of lead and pinched it between the two tips. Carefully, I worked the bullet out. With Sten's larger Bowie, I cauterized the wound. I pressed hard and the flesh sizzled. Better to burn deep and get the blood to stop.

Rather than move him, I let him lay in the clean loose sand. I made a pillow with his saddle and spread his saddle blanket over him. I took a canteen and wet his lips and poured the water over his burned wound. Already his face flushed red with fever. I would stay here and care for him. His size made it impossible to do anything else.

My constant worry was the attention Gertrude showed Sten. She kept lowering her muzzle and snuffling into his face. I led her off and tied her securely to a tree. She fought the reins. Slowly she calmed down, content to stand and watch.

The fever continued for several days. I managed to shoot a rabbit, and in a pan I added water and made a broth. I spoon fed him. Some of it went down but most spilled or was coughed out. I kept trying. On the third day his fever broke, and Sten managed to pull himself up on one elbow. That Norwegian had the stamina of ten men.

"No, Darrell," Sten kept saying as I tried to push him back down.

"Hush now and stay quiet," I urged.

"I got to tell you what happened."

"You just take it easy. Don't talk."

Awake, it was much easier to get broth and water into him. He even managed to eat some of the rabbit.

"You got to go after the cattle!" Sten kept saying over and over.

Against my better judgment, I finally left him laying there, guarded by Gertrude, while I went for the cattle. It was either that, or have the lad stand up and try to go with me. That would certainly break his wound open. So I went alone. I found the three dead men. The cattle were scattered and I followed their tracks. After two days, I managed to come back with fourteen. I was glad to have them and I was able to herd them along and down into that arroyo. When I arrived, that fool of a boy was trying to sit up.

"Lay down, lad! You got another two weeks before you try that!"

"But I got to help you!"

"Son, how you going to inherit my ranch and these cattle, if you bleed to death?" I shouted down at him over the din of the herd.

Gertrude kept running in circles, chasing bellowing critters away from Sten.

I dismounted and walked up to the boy. He laid there, his mouth open in surprise and both hands pushing flat into the sand in the act of trying to get up.

"Well, son," I said. "Don't sit there with your mouth open. Flies will get in."

I swear, two grown men never did smile such silly grins.

*1st Printing, *STORYTELLER: Canada's Fiction Magazine*, Vol.13/Issue 4 *(2007)*

NUISANCE AND THE GIRL

The wind blew hard all winter. The temperature didn't go much above zero for months. Snow fell and piled up higher than the roof. Doors froze and so did I, and so did my horse in the shed next door. When I finally got out to feed my mount, it was frozen solid and laying on its side. Sure felt bad about losing him. I thought about the work it would take to get the carcass out of there before it began to rot in the spring—if spring and warm weather ever did come.

The thaw came in a wild rush. The air turned and with it a warm wind that melted the snow all at once. Water flowed everywhere down the mountain. Rivers gorged themselves with muddy runoff and overflowed their steep banks. The rushing torrents dislodged rocks, trees, and trails. Water flooded places it hadn't been in a hundred years. Tons of earth and rock were moved and piled up every which way. New trails would have to be found to get off the mountain. I took care of the horse and that was a gruesome job. I vowed I would never winter with a beast of burden again. I still had my dog, Nuisance. He stayed loyal and by my side. I swear, without him, I would have frozen in that shack.

That winter was so severe I had cabin fever like no other time in my life. Once the flowers and green grass sprung up, I howled like a wolf at my freedom. I couldn't wait to get to town. Nuisance found the way through the jumble of rock. It was like the mountain had transformed itself. On a lower meadow where aspen and a forest of ponderosa pine had been, there was nothing left but bare rock. In that bedrock, I saw a yellow streak and discovered the richest pocket of gold I'd ever seen. I forgot all about town. In my fever, I went back for a pickaxe and dug up that yellow stuff and hid it away. I had enough to set me up for the rest of my life, if I was careful. It put a new perspective on things.

"Well, Nuisance," I told the dog. "What you want most in your life? A big juicy ham bone? A soft stuffed bed to lie on? A female? A fancy studded collar? You tell me, boy!"

All that dog did was stare with shiny black eyes, twist his head, and bark. So much for a pal who didn't need but a bit of food and a good scratch.

We made our way down the mountain with a fraction of that gold. In the past I panned a few ounces, so turning this in for money wouldn't raise any eyebrows—I hoped. First thing I did was go to the assayer's office. I walked out with a few hundred dollars. Turned in the pelts I brought down, and they fetched a bit more. Now I had money like never before.

I bought me a shiny new rifle. My first new one. The fanciest and the best they had. One with a scope on it and could hold a number of shells and shoot a long way. Then

I bought all the can goods a good mule could carry, and with it the mule to haul them. Next, I got myself a new outfit from head to toe. I bought some fancy duds and work clothes, good heavy wool. The most I ever owned. The stable man held the mule and my stash for me. In the clothes, I hid away a little extra cash.

My next move was my first mistake. Old Nuisance and me went into a bar for a little drink. What trouble we found in there would last a lifetime. I was happy and wanted to buy a few rounds. Another mistake.

"Bar keep!" I shouted. "Drinks for everybody!"

It was the middle of the day and the ten folks or so in the place were sort of lazing about. When I shouted free drinks they woke up and stampeded the bar. Money seemed to be scarce, except on me. After the first few drinks of hard stuff followed by beer, I don't rightly recollect what happened. Towards evening all I remember is a piano and a banjo, a woman singing, and a couple old saloon gals hanging on me. A crowd of men cheered me on like I was their long lost friend. Things sort of blurred after that.

Old Nuisance's whining and wet tongue woke me up. I was laying in some trash in the back alley. I squinted in the bright sunlight and looked around. First thing I noticed, my pockets were all turned inside out. I'd been drugged and rolled like a greenhorn fool.

"Are you alright, Mister?" asked a gal who stared down at me.

She was a skinny little thing and she looked hungry and lost. Like she didn't belong in this mountain town. She was holding a carpetbag and her dress hung lopsided and was too big for her. I squinted up at her and wondered. She looked sort of familiar.

"Who are...what?" I mumbled with a mouth that didn't taste right.

I tried to get up and my head ached just awful. With every movement, there were shooting pains.

"Ohhhh!" I groaned.

"Serves you right," said the gal. "A grown man throwing his hard earned money around like you did. Don't you know, Mister, they took it all?"

"Who?"

"All those people did. When you passed out they went through your pockets like hungry rats."

"Who are you?"

"Don't you remember?"

I stared at her some more.

"Oh yeah, you're the singer."

"I was. The owner of the saloon told me to cozy up to you and see what I could get. When I refused, he fired me."

"He did, did he?" I started to get an anger up.

"You can't do anything," the girl cautioned. "Those men working for him would knock you sillier than you are now."

"Look, lady," I began.

"Oh, never mind," said the girl. "I came to see if you were still living. You are, so I'll go."

"Lady," I said. "Could you help me up?"

She gave me a hand, but there wasn't much of her and I nearly pulled her over. Instead, I let go and got to my feet.

"Ohhhh," I groaned and held my broken head.

"It's what you deserve," said the girl. "If I thought you could, I'd ask you to buy me lunch. Me being fired, no money, and no place to go."

I remembered my pack of clothing and my little stash. The stable wasn't far and I asked her to walk with me.

"Well?" said the girl when we got there.

The owner saw me and laughed. I found my bundle and took out the cash. Good thing I saved some of it. That little filly was still waiting outside when I returned. She was petting Nuisance. That dog NEVER played up to no one else and I took a second look at the girl. If she was wearing decent clothes and fixed her hair, she might be a looker. As it was, wearing that big bag of a dress and tussled hair, she looked silly.

My head still hurt, but I managed to put away a steak, a big slice of ham, some bacon, and six eggs. I followed that with a pot of coffee. The girl sat with big round black eyes and just stared. She sort of pecked at her food and I watched her drink half a cup of coffee and put down an egg or two. No wonder she was such a skinny little thing. I never talked much when I was eating. When I finished, I worked at holding down a big belch. I couldn't, so I turned my head, covered my mouth, and it just ripped out of me.

"Excuse me!" I said.

"Well," said the girl, exposing the snow whites of her eyes. "You seem to be a man of big appetites. I sure hope you can pay for all this."

"Don't worry, I can."

"Mister Frankie Benjamin, after seeing you spend more money than I ever saw in my life, I don't know how you could have another red cent to your name."

"How's come you know my name?"

My head was feeling better. I looked around the little restaurant and saw that all the customers were eyeing us. The counter and nearly every table was filled with patrons. You see, I was a big strapping man and I just naturally gathered that kind of attention. I lowered my voice.

"How's come?" I asked again.

"Well," said the girl. "You shouted it out twenty times in the bar last night. You kept throwing out wads of money and telling everybody they was your friend, and to just call you old Frankie Benjamin."

"I guess I was feeling my oats," I said.

"Having that headache is what you deserve," said the girl. "But there was no call for all those folks to rob you. That was evil."

"Say," I said, getting interested. "What's your name and your story?"

"I'm Vera," said the girl, getting her nose up. "And my story, as you put it, is none of your business!"

Offended, the girl made to get up. I put out a big hand and grabbed her arm. More gently, I tugged on it.

"Sorry," I said. "Stay and we'll talk some."

I stared at her and waited for her to speak. I guess I was rude and had no real familiarity with girls, me being a mountain man and all and never having much truck with people. She looked at me with those big eyes of hers.

"If you must know," she said. "I came here looking for my uncle. My folks died a while back and I left a job in Pueblo to get here. My uncle and I corresponded some, and he asked me to visit. By the time I got here, he died. I tried talking to my cousins, but they thought I was after his things and…"

"And you ran out of money and got a job singing in that bar."

"Yes. Singing was the only respectable thing that man offered me. Then you came in throwing all that money around."

"I'm sorry you lost your job," I said.

We sat in silence and drank coffee. I thought some on what I could do for her, and my mind was blank. Only people I knew were the assayer, the stable owner, and the proprietor of the general store. Then a thought struck me.

"Stay here," I said and I threw down some coins. "Drink your coffee and if they ask, pay them with this. I'll be right back."

She opened her mouth to speak and I was gone.

The owner of the general store didn't want a clerk. He said he didn't have enough business and that his children and wife took up the slack. Then I got to thinking about all that money I had. I took the owner aside and began to explain about the girl, how nice she was and how she needed a break. I gave that man a chunk of money and told him to keep ten percent and pay the girl with the rest of it. The owner shook his head and then finally, reluctantly, agreed.

"I'd have to meet her first," he said. "Then I'll decide for sure. Can't have just anybody taking a room in my house and working in my store."

I went and got Vera. When I explained what it was

about, she smiled. It was a smile I would never forget. It worked out. I said my goodbyes, took my mule and supplies, and went up the mountain to home.

* * *

That winter was the mildest we had in the ten years I spent up on the mountain. I loved these mountains and nothing could tear me away from them. Or, so I thought. I was near thirty and I learned a long time ago that I needed space to live.

All winter long, petting and hugging that fool dog, I thought of that slip of a girl. I didn't ask, so I had no idea how old she was. Twenty, if I had to guess. Most girls as pretty as her were married soon as they hit their teens. Wondered why she wasn't. She did have a bossy streak to her. Maybe not so bossy, as independent. Anyway, all winter long I thought about her. In the spring I couldn't wait to make my way down. I had a lot of pelts to stack on the mule, and there was that gold.

First place I went was to drop off the pelts. Then at the stable I sort of asked about Vera. That stable man, he just laughed.

"Saw you had an eye for her," he said.

"Dang it, man! Just answer the question. Is she working at the general store?"

"Prettiest lady in the whole town. Once Peterson and his wife helped the little thing, why, she cleaned up real nice. Filled out some, too. Boys here abouts line up every weekend at the store just to get a look at her. Saturday night, poor thing gets all tuckered out dancing with them young men."

The barber had a bathhouse in the back. I brought my good clothes. Had me a bath, shaved off my beard for the first time in ten years, and had my hair trimmed. The barber put some fancy smelling stuff on me, slicked my hair, and when I looked in the mirror, I didn't recognize the feller looking back. I wasn't completely ugly. Dark hair, dark eyes, and all.

When I walked in the store, I could feel my face redden up. Nothing I could do about it and I was angry at myself. Had no idea what was going on with me. Nuisance tried to follow me in and I used that as an excuse to go back outside. Before I left, I saw a good looking woman in a print dress at the counter. Her dark hair was long and smooth around a pretty white face. I saw those eyes flashing and I thought for a moment they stared at me. It was the weekend and just like the stable man said, young men were standing around picking up any fool thing to buy.

I ran into Peterson out on the porch. He was all smiles and extended a welcome hand. I shook it.

"Well, Mr. Benjamin," he said. "I see you made it out of the mountains. I'm glad to see you. Vera turned out to be the best thing my store ever had. Ever since she started working here, business has been booming. Men come from miles away to see her and they just naturally pick up something to buy. I thought about it and I'm giving you your money back."

I grabbed his arm, pulled him close, and looked him hard in the eye.

"Not necessary, Peterson," I whispered. "And, not so

loud. I'm glad she's getting along."

"Getting along?" said Peterson still smiling. "My worry is when she gets married and leaves."

That did it. With Nuisance by my side, we walked down the street and went into the restaurant Vera and I ate at the year before. I thought about the bar, but I didn't want to go through that again.

Drink didn't settle with me. Only a fool would return there.

I ordered food and sat there and pecked at it. First time in my life I wasn't hungry. What was wrong with me? I stepped outside with the plate and gave it all to Nuisance. When the restaurant man complained, I gave him a tip. Then I sauntered back down the street and out of town.

Nuisance was by my side and knowing something was wrong, he whined. I petted him and found a rock to sit on. My mountain loomed high above me. The peaks still glistened with snow. Up the sides of lower mountains, grew millions of cedar and piñon. Below, in the rolling foothills, the grass was still green. Soon it would fade and turn yellow. Beyond the village, the prairie extended to far horizons. It was what endeared me to the land—these endless views. I sat and petted my dog.

"What's wrong with me, Nuisance?" I asked.

He made a high pitched whine and then licked my hand. He knew I was hurting.

On the way back to the stable I saw a sign on one of the store windows. It advertised a Saturday night dance and on Sunday, a box lunch picnic. The lunches would go to the highest bidder along with the girl or woman who made them.

Tomorrow would be Saturday. I wondered if I had the gumption to go to the dance. I hadn't danced with a girl since the eighth grade except a couple times with my mother, before she passed. I needed a new shirt and tie. Normally I would have gone to the general store. Instead, I found what I needed at a dressmaker's shop that advertised men's shirts.

The dance was crowded. I could see everything from my hotel window across the street. This was the first time I didn't bed down in the stable. I looked out the window for a while and then lay on the bed. The music started and the night advanced. At dark I again looked out the window. The outside of the hall was crowded with men and women getting air. The music kept on and on. Finally, I couldn't stand it anymore. I went down the stairs and out of the hotel.

I had to push my way onto the crowded dance floor. There were couples of all ages swirling in a circle. Many of the men worked hard at it. Sweat glistened on their faces under the lantern light. On a platform performed a piano, banjo, several guitars, a clarinet, and a trumpet. Below the musicians, couples danced in their very best.

It took a while, but I saw her. She had filled out and the dress she wore complimented her figure. She was still very slim but not like when I first met her. Her hair was long and flowing, down to her shoulders, held in place by a red ribbon. Her dark eyes flashed as I remembered and she was smiling with red lips. Her skin was flawless and white and I stared boldly. I was not the only one. Men and boys of all ages had their eyes on the prettiest girl in the room, and it was Vera.

I stood there and my heart beat faster. I felt all kinds of jealous thoughts. Who was I to think this way? A recluse, a trapper, a lonely old mountain man who was ten years her senior? I had no claim on her. Just before I turned to go, she saw me. She appeared to be startled and then she smiled directly at me. It was a radiant smile. I waved and smiled back.

The dance stopped. A line of men and boys stood before Vera and tried to talk to her. I watched. She turned from them, having to tug her hands free, and pushed through the crowd towards me.

"Hello, Frankie Benjamin," she said.

She stood close and looked up at me. I had to bend nearer to hear her in the noise of the crowd.

"Hello, Vera," I answered.

There were so many things I wanted to say.

"It's hot," she shouted. "Shall we go outside?"

Somehow we made our way through the crowd and out onto the street. Men and boys followed and I heard her making polite comments. When they would not take no for an answer, she pushed away from her suitors and grabbed my arm. I was thrilled and my heart pounded in reaction to her grasp. We walked together down the street and stood in the dark. Her admirers stared in consternation at who she was with.

"Now" she said. "At last we can talk."

"You seem to be very popular."

"Don't pay any attention to that. It was your kindness,

your getting me that job with Mr. and Mrs. Peterson at the general store that did all this."

"Yes?" that's all I could think to say.

"I wanted to thank you. Mrs. Peterson has helped me. Taught me manners and social graces."

"I'm happy for you," I heard myself murmur.

"I thought about you all winter," she said. "I wondered what you were doing up there on that mountain, what it was like to stay through the cold and snow. I wondered if you did well with your traps. If I would see you again this spring."

"I'm here."

"Yes, did you have a good year?"

"One of my best. It was a mild winter and I was able to get out and about. The traps were full and I did well."

"I am so glad," said Vera, and then she laughed.

All this time she held onto my arm. When she let go, I felt like reaching out for her hand, but was afraid to do so. Me, Frankie Benjamin, over six feet, two hundred pounds. I still dwarfed this little girl, and for that matter, every other person in that mountain town.

"Vera!" came men's voices from across the street. "Vera, come on! You owe us dances!"

"Do you dance, Frankie?" she asked.

"No," I lied. "I never learned."

"Oh," she responded.

She sounded forlorn and hesitant.

"I must go back," she said. "Mrs. Peterson said it was my social duty to dance with all the eligible men. That until…"

"I see."

My pulse raced and my head ached. I was petrified and struck dumb. I couldn't think of anything to say.

"Tomorrow," she said. "Tomorrow there is a box lunch social and a picnic. Perhaps…"

"I'll be there," I said without thinking.

"Oh, I am so glad, Frankie," she smiled up at me.

She suddenly took hold of my upper right arm. Her hands could only circle part of it. It felt wonderful. Then she ran across the street and disappeared into the crowd.

I ambled back to the hotel and Nuisance slept while I paced. I embarrassed even myself with my own outlandish thoughts. I stayed awake most of the night. I awakened early and fully aware. My first thought was that I would not make a fool of myself and go to the picnic. She would not want me to bid against all those men and boys. Certainly she would be as embarrassed as I was at the thought of doing so. What could a trapper offer such a beauty as her? She could never love the mountains, the isolation, the way I did.

I poked at my breakfast. Nuisance ate what I could not. The dog was going to get fat. I paced the rest of the day. I took a long walk outside of town. I returned. Nuisance watched while I primped before the mirror. I nearly paced a hole in the floor of the hotel. When it came time, I rushed out of the room, adjusting my string tie and jacket one last time.

The box lunches of the married women went first. Husbands bid on their wife's meal. A few bachelors made a bid and the crowd laughed in amusement. The single women's lunches went next. Vera's was held for the very last. I should have known, as everyone in town knew, that this was the culmination of the event. Yes, up on that mountain I read books and I knew a few big words.

When Vera's time came, fifty cents went to a dollar and then two. Ten dollars advanced to twenty. When it got to a month's pay of thirty, there seemed to be only two bidders left. When it reached thirty-five, I spoke up.

"Fifty dollars!" I blurted out and then turned red.

Everyone in the crowd stared at me. I looked up at Vera, who sat on the platform with her picnic basket on the table before her. To my astonishment, Vera did not seem to be embarrassed. She smiled and brought her basket to me. The two of us walked away.

"I am so happy," Vera teased. "It must mean that you think very well of me to pay so much money for my lunch. You don't even know if I can cook."

"That's alright," I said. "If you can't, I know how."

"Well!" she complained.

I was starting off badly.

It turned out that her chicken did taste good. And so did her apple pie. We talked and joked through the rest of the afternoon.

"Frankie, may I ask you a question?"

"Yes?"

"Did you think about me this past winter?"

"Some," I said.

"Oh, you!" she protested and punched me in the arm.

I grabbed hold of her in playful defense and before I knew what was happening we kissed. After that, the words tumbled out of both of us.

* * *

The snow hasn't started yet. The wind is beginning to blow cold on the mountain and our little cabin. Soon the blizzards will come and there will be no way down off the mountain. Vera is sitting on the hill, enjoying the view, with Nuisance by her side. I cannot believe that out of all those young men who were after her, she married me. She said she would give a winter a try, and if she liked it, we would stay up here. If not, I agreed to follow her down and both of us would return each spring. I hope I can give her a happy life. I haven't told her yet, but it's a comfort to have the gold put away, for a time of need.

OLD MAN IN A ROCKING CHAIR

I first spotted the old man when he came riding into Colorado City on a lame paint. His gear was faded and worn. When he sold horse, saddle, and bridle to the hostler at the livery, not much money was exchanged. Everything about him was well used—including himself. He was a tough old man, the leathery kind. He had a face weathered by the sun, and it looked like he had lived a hard life and earned every wrinkle. There sure were a lot of them.

School was over for the summer and I was helping Ma and Pa at the store. I was sweeping the porch when I first saw the stranger and figured he was an old frontiersman stopping for supplies. I was surprised when he sold his horse and gear, and even more surprised when he entered the store carrying the advertisement. He walked right up to the counter and spoke to Pa. Old, he may have been, but there was a spry way about him. He was wearing a wide sombrero, a stained buckskin shirt and yellow neckerchief, worn corduroy pants, and big old boots. On his hips he wore a wide belt with a pistol and a large skinning knife.

"This here cabin still for sale?" asked the oldster.

"Why sure, stranger," answered Pa. "You fixin' to live here?"

"I reckon it'll be my last stand," the old man commented. "Says here a hunnerd dollars. That include a well and a hunnerd feet on both sides?"

"Yes, sir," answered my Pa curiously.

"That there place fit to live in?"

"It needs some work. Some cleaning and repairing. But the roof's sound."

"How do I see it?"

"My son's there on the porch. He'll take you down and show you. We don't keep it locked."

That old man walked out on the porch and focused his gray eyes on me. I felt as if he took my measure and summed me up before ever speaking.

"Well, boy. You gonna sweep or show me your Pa's cabin?"

"I'll, I'll," I stammered.

"Well, spit it out, boy."

"I'll show it to you, sir."

Seems like on that walk down to the far end of town the old man put me at my ease, I never stuttered in his presence again. He asked me a lot of questions and, being that it was a small stamping mill town for the mines, I knew everybody and everything he asked. He mentioned needing supplies. I told him Ma and Pa charged fair prices and would appreciate his business.

We made it to the cabin, and he took a walk around the outside. After a long gander at the mountains behind, he commented on the view. Then he tried the well, and the pump wouldn't suck. I told him Pa would fix it. The old man pushed hard on the warped back door and entered.

We walked around in the dust of the two room cabin. I was plumb embarrassed at the condition of the place.

"I'll help you fix it up, mister," I said. "Sorry it's so dusty dirty. No one's been in it for a year."

"Well, that's right neighborly of you, boy," he answered.

"My names Teddy," I told him. "Short for Theodore. Pa named me after Roosevelt."

"Right glad to know yeah, Teddy," responded the old man.

He shook my hand and his grip was rock solid. It made me feel respected and all growed up. We walked back to the store and I was afraid he wouldn't buy the cabin. I wanted to get to know this strange man, and I was delighted when he laid out five twenty dollar gold pieces on my Pa's counter.

"I want you to throw in this boy for a few days cleaning. I'll be buying supplies and I'll especially be wantin that there rocker you got outside on the porch."

"Why sure, ah...Mister...?"

"Haven't been called by my right name since I was a youngster," said the old man. "Some folks have called and known me by a lot of names. Now the Injuns, they had a way of naming a man. The Cheyenne used to call me Big Man Walking. The Crows, well, let's just say they had a harder one. Heck, one names good as another. Supposin you just call me Sandy."

And that was the introduction the old man made to our little town.

After him and me fixed up that cabin, it looked right homey. We became good friends, and I took to spending all my free time down there. He was most interesting, and the things he had seen and done were better than any stories out of some book. His talk was more thrilling than the school marm's. When I told Ma and Pa, they just sort of stared at each other, and put hands to their mouths. They didn't believe his tales. But I did.

Sometimes I felt that what he was saying was so important it should be written down. At night, lying in my bed, I wondered that I should know a man who had lived so long—a man who had met so many famous people. He was like a walking history book. Why he had known just about everybody. He spoke of Kit Carson, Jedediah Smith, Uncle Dick Wooten, Black Kettle, all sorts of folks. There was no telling how old that man was, but he had lived a long time. He talked about being afeared of dying with his boots off. The way he went on, I wondered if he was ashamed he had survived.

"Teddy, it ain't fittin for a man to grow so old he can't do for himself. I was afeared of this. My mammy and folks lived to more'n a hunnerd years old. Never dreamed it would happen to me."

Sandy took to sitting in that rocker, with his face full to the hot sun. He would sit for hours and stare off across to the Greenhorn and Wet Mountains. Each day I would come and see him there. Sometimes I wasn't sure he was still breathing. He liked to bake those old bones of his. One day, I came to ask and listen for another story. He was sitting there, like always, staring off at the mountains. I kept thinking he was still as death. And that time, he was.

*1st Printing, *ROPE AND WIRE,* August 2008

LITTLE SAMMY TUCKER AND THE STRANGERS

Eight-year-old Sammy dashed down the narrow path between the two picket fences, ducked and opened a loose board, and crawled quickly in the hole in the hedge. He sat down and caught his breath, sucking in air until his lungs stopped burning and his heart ceased pounding. The strangers who had come into town were after someone and that was obvious to the boy. Sammy knew every house, every picket fence, every nook and cranny in town, and every hiding place. Out playing on this Saturday morning, Sammy had watched the first dark stranger ride in, dismount, and slowly make his way up the alley, using all the cover of the hedges, fences, and buildings. Sammy had watched this dusty stranger and noted his two tied-down guns.

Sammy had then carefully made the circuit of the town and from his many hiding places had watched three more darkly dressed, heavily armed men, come in from the other three directions. They tied off their horses and then advanced towards the center of town, keeping themselves hidden and out of sight. Sammy watched the fourth and final man from the hedge behind old Mrs. Lally's house.

The stranger walked cautiously up the alley directly past the boy. The only items on the gunman that were not grimy and dusty were his heavily oiled belt and holsters and his two gleaming pistols.

The tall figure disappeared around a corner. The boy's stomach rumbled and he remembered Mrs. Lally's raspberries. He spied the heavily laden bushes that lay just inside the hedge. Sammy quickly picked and crammed the ripe luscious berries into his mouth as fast as he could. Satisfying his craving, he wiped his mouth with the back of his hand and managed to spread the red stain across his lips and cheeks. The boy ran to the water pump behind the house and gave it a couple cranks. He stuck his head down and caught the cold flowing liquid in his mouth and swallowed. He repeated the process several times, finally quenching his hearty thirst.

From the back door of the house Sammy heard a creak of hinges and the twang of the long spring. There stood Mrs. Lally herself. The boy ran for the hole in the hedge, dove through it, and fled into the alley. As he rose and was dashing away, he heard the old lady.

"I know who you are, Sammy Tucker, and it won't do you no good to run once I tell your ma! You leave my raspberries alone this year. Ya hear?"

The voice faded as Sammy ran as hard as he could straight up the alley and towards the center of town. It was June and a very hot day for the sleepy little town of Aguilar, Colorado. It was near noon and already the temperature was over ninety. There was little wind and dust rose up from under the boy's bare feet as he ran across the hot dry sand. Coming to the corner where the last gunman had disappeared, Sammy skidded to a stop and peered around a hedge. The man, looking out from under his sombrero, was still walking cautiously along, his hands near his two guns. Sammy watched the man turn another corner and disappear into a narrow dark alley between the town's hotel, and general store, both of which faced the main street.

Determined now, the boy ran straight up the path between the gun shop and barber shop and onto Main Street. Looking both ways, he headed for the small jail, a low adobe hut standing across the wide dusty street. Sammy ran with all his might until he came to the dark open doorway. He skidded into the cool shade of the small building. Sitting at a scarred old desk with his feet up was Deputy Sheriff Juan Sanchez.

"Juan," breathed the boy heavily. "There's four strangers in town. They're gunman and hiding between the buildings along Main Street."

"How many times do I have to tell you, it's Deputy Sanchez. What game are you up to now?"

"I'm telling you, four gunmen came riding in, each from a different direction. They tied their horses off and came up through the alleyways. I tell you they are after someone. Come on, I'll show you where they're hiding."

"I'm not playing one of your fairytale games. What's that you got smeared all over your face? You into Mrs. Lally's raspberries again? What did I tell you about that?"

"Deputy Sanchez, you got to believe me. There are four gunmen hiding between the buildings of Main Street and they're waiting to shoot someone."

"I told you, I'm not playing any games. You get along with yourself, and stay away from those raspberries!"

"Juan, you're a lazy, good-for-nuthin deputy. You just wait and see if I'm not telling the truth."

"Sammy!" said the deputy slamming his feet to the rough wooden floor and standing up. "If I get my hands on you, I'm going to tan your butt! You get yourself out of here and I mean now!"

The deputy advanced towards the boy and extended both his arms in earnest. Sammy ducked and ran out of the small office and jail. He turned and stopped just outside the door and yelled.

"You just wait, Mr. Deputy. Someone is going to get gunned down and when people find out you knew and didn't do nothing to stop it. Well, you'll see!"

"Git!" shouted the angry man.

The deputy, in disgust, shifted his belt and floppy holster with the heavy pistol. He watched Sammy Tucker disappear between the barber shop and the gun shop.

"Darn kid," growled the deputy.

Having second thoughts, Juan stepped out of the cool jail, onto the boardwalk, and into the bright hot sun. Looking up and down the quiet street, he saw nothing out of order. In anger, he headed for Sophie's Café. A cup of coffee and a bite to eat would sooth his rankled disposition. *That Sammy is nothing but trouble. Someday he's going to grow up into a real problem if someone doesn't put a stop to his mischief.*

"Darn, dumb, deputy sheriff!" mumbled Sammy.

Sammy ran between the buildings and stopped in the cool shade. He slid down with his back against the gun shop wall.

Now what do I do? he thought. *Who are those men after? Whoever it is, that person better be warned. What chance does he have against four gunmen? Gunslingers don't hardly ever come here anymore.*

Sammy sat in the cool of the shade looking out onto Main Street. The gunmen were in hiding as if they were waiting for someone to ride in. The back of town faced the pass through the mountains and several of the mountain ranches. Perhaps it was from that direction the rider would come.

The boy ran back down the alley, past Mrs. Lally's house, and continued on. He turned west and ran around the outside of town. He reached the stable that stood facing the mountains at the end of the village. There, the excited boy ran to a water trough and cranked the handle. He ducked his head under the spout and drank thirstily. This was dry work and a hot day.

From the west came a dark dusty rider. The boy turned and noticed the newest member of their community. This was the stranger who had bought the Gonzales Ranch up on the side of the mountain where Gonzales Creek flowed. It was high beautiful country, isolated, and far from town, and where the elk and mule deer ran. This stranger had come from nowhere and paid cash for three hundred and twenty acres. No one knew anything about the stranger or where he came from. His name was Tom Teeple and he was a quiet man who looked like he could take care of himself, and who appeared to be able to handle that pistol he wore. Here was someone those gunmen might be after. Sammy took a chance and ran up to the dark mustang the rancher was riding.

"Mr. Teeple, there are strangers in town. They look like gunmen and are hiding between the buildings along Main Street."

The rider stopped his mount and looked down at the small boy in dusty and faded bib overalls, and bare feet.

"Did you tell the deputy?"

"Yes sir, but he didn't believe me and didn't do nothin."

"Where are the men?"

Teeple began to dismount and, as he did, he flipped the reins from around the horse's neck. Once his feet struck the ground he took the two reins in his left hand, and stood looking down at the boy. With his right hand he pushed back his sombrero. Sammy looked up and could see the blue eyes in the dark tanned face of the older man.

"There's one between the hotel and the general store, there's another directly across the street near Sophie's Café and Mrs. Humphry's dress shop. The other two are back down the street near the saloon and across from each other. It looks like an ambush."

"What are they dressed like?"

"All dark clothes. One's wearing a duster even in the heat. And, mister, all four of em, are wearing two guns apiece."

"You got real sharp eyes, sonny. What's your name?"

The small boy pulled himself erect and looked up seriously at the tall rancher.

"It's Samuel Tucker, but everybody calls me Sammy."

"Well, Sammy, here's a dollar. Now you run along and stay out of the way. And, son, thanks for the warning."

"Is it you they're after?"

"Could be."

"What are you going to do? There's four of them!"

"I'm going to do what I came here for—buy some things at the general store and eat at Sophie's Café. Now you run along and stay off the street."

Sammy walked slowly back to the water trough and watched as the tall quiet man reached into his saddle bag and pulled out an extra pistol and slipped it down under his front belt. Then the rancher stepped forward, holding the horse's head. He walked beside the dark horse, and allowed it to be a shield, at least from one side. Mr. Teeple held the reins with his left hand; his right was down and close to his pistol. Sammy thought he saw the man's fingers slip down and loosen the leather thong from the pistol's hammer. Then, the boy ran across the street and, as fast as he could, he cut around the blacksmith shop, quiet in the hot day sun. He ran behind the building and raced down a side street. Nothing in the world was going to stop the boy from sneaking up to where the two gunmen were waiting.

Sammy ran as fast as he ever had in his life. His lungs burned and his sides ached as he made his way to a place opposite the hotel. He ran down between an abandoned, rundown building and the mercantile. There was a high porch in front of the mercantile and a hole under the porch. Silently, the boy ducked and scooted into the space beneath the porch. He lay down on his stomach in the dust and watched for the rancher to come into view.

Sammy waited, his heart pounded and his breath came fast. Despite the coolness of the porch the boy was warm, and he absent-mindedly wiped the sweat from his forehead. He tried to slow his breathing, but his heart still pounded with pent up excitement. Just when he thought the rancher wasn't coming, and had turned off, he saw him approach. From between the next buildings, Sammy clearly saw one of the gunmen come out. Because of the rancher and his horse, Sammy couldn't see the other man across the street.

"That's far enough, Teeple," said the man Sammy could see.

"Hello, Frank," said Teeple. "You and your clan looking for me?"

"You killed my brother up in Leadville, and now we're going to kill you."

"It was a fair fight, Frank."

"Don't matter. He was my brother, and the Rivett family don't never let that go."

Sammy could see the man called Frank reach down and draw his right hand pistol. The boy looked back at the rancher and it seemed like he waited and then at the last moment raised his hand and drew. His pistol exploded once and then twice. The stranger, Frank, jerked violently back and crimson appeared on his dark shirt front. The man's gun went off and the bullet went harmlessly into the dust in front of him. Sammy watched as the gunman fell and then there was another gunshot. The horse that the rancher was holding screamed, raised its two front legs, and then tore the reins from Teeple's hands and raced off down the street. The boy could see the other gunman standing with pistol in hand. The man fired and the boy could hear the whump of the bullet as it struck the rancher. Teeple staggered back—he'd been hit on his left side.

The boy then saw the rancher fire two more shots, sounding nearly as one, and the dark stranger across the street staggered, reached for his head, and fell forward onto his face.

Sammy looked up the street. The last two gunmen came running, guns in hand. One of the men had two pistols and he was firing each one steadily as he came. Teeple held his gun up and carefully aimed and fired at the man with the two pistols. His shot seemed to miss. He pulled back the hammer, aimed, and the boy heard the hammer click on an empty chamber. Sammy watched the rancher holster the empty pistol and then draw the other one from his waist. A bullet nicked him high up on his right shoulder, and Sammy watched as Mr. Teeple set himself and again aimed and fired. This time the man with the two guns jerked and went down. The firing stopped.

"I see you got Frank and Cousin Jim—and now Michael. But you ain't getting me before I put you down."

"You always did talk too much, Mort. If you're going to shoot, get it over with."

The boy could smell the smoke of the burnt gunpowder and taste the dust. Time stood still as he watched the two men raise their pistols and fire. Both men missed and then fired repeatedly. Sammy could see the gunman, Mort, stagger as each bullet struck him.

There was a splattering of bullets behind him in the

street and then the last gunman slipped and fell to his knees, his pistol falling into the dirt. The boy's eyes went back to the rancher and he could see another wound high up on his right thigh. Sammy slid out from under the porch and ran into the street. The rancher turned, gun in hand, and seeing the boy, held his fire.

"Kid, I nearly shot you."

"Mister Teeple, I saw the whole thing."

"Yeah, well if it keeps you away from guns, maybe it's a good thing."

"Are they all dead?"

"If they aren't, they will be."

"You're hurt, Mr. Teeple. I'll run and get the doctor."

"No, I think he's probably on his way. Here, help me get to that porch and sit down."

Sammy came near. The rancher put down his right hand and leaned heavily on the boy's shoulder and limped to the porch steps where he slowly and painfully sat down.

"Here, help me bind this wound on my leg," said the rancher as he pulled his bandanna from around his neck.

The boy did as he was told. People came out of the shops all up and down the street. The youngster and the rancher both watched as Deputy Sheriff Juan Sanchez came running up, gun in his right hand.

"What's going on here?" demanded the deputy, breathing heavily.

"What do you think, Sammy?" said the rancher. "Shouldn't the deputy here be looking for a new job?"

*1st Printing, *THE LAKESHORE GUARDIAN,* September 2007

THE DUST STILL RISING

The old man and the boy sat on the edge of the porch overlooking the hard scrabble farm. It was mostly dry, western Colorado land irrigated by a small creek that failed to run in the drought years. Several miles due west, the shining face of the Front Range of the Rockies stood high and majestic in the clear pale blue sky. Their jagged tips still covered with snow. Across the barren yard was the barn and next to it a corral with several horses ambling idly about under the hot sun. The old man and boy were in shade and a warm breeze wafted across their faces as they spoke to each other.

"Is it true, Grandpa?" asked the boy looking up into the weathered face of the gnarled old man. "All those stories you told me?"

"As true as me sitting right in front of you, lad," answered the old man obviously irritated. "Has your Pa been telling you different?"

The boy looked up, too startled to answer, a guilty frown written on his face.

"Don't you pay no attention to what your Pa says about me, boy," responded the old man with vigor. "He's got a big mad on against me for never being around when he was growing up. It don't look like he's ever gonna git over it."

"Pa says that I should keep my nose to the grindstone, that what you say is malarkey."

"He said all that? What else?"

"He says you were a no account and always will be, and that I shouldn't pay no attention to what you have to say."

The old man rose angrily from the porch and grabbed the boy by his shoulders with sinewy hands that gripped with surprising strength. The fingers went into the boy's muscles and the sudden pain bit deep.

"Now you listen here, boy. I've been yarnin on you these past few days and I admit some of those stories were stretched a bit, but not one of em was made up, and every thing I told you is sitten on a foundation of truth. You hear me? Don't let your Pa go stompin on my life. What I have to share with you is history, boy—family history and my life and my experiences. Your Pa mayn't care but you do, don't you, lad?"

The old man's hands gripped harder and he shook the boy's shoulders with the question.

"Well?"

"Yes, Sir," the boy nodded.

"What I got to tell you, son, is a heap, cause I traveled and lived hard. Unlike your Pa, I had a fire in my heart and a yearnin to see the wide open spaces. I stomped from one corner of this country to the other in a time when this land was wide open. You ain't never gonna meet no living hombre like your grandpa, never again. If'n I don't tell, my life dies with me, and you won't never know what I saw and done. Don't let your Pa stand in the way. You are my blood, my grandson, and I got the right."

Again, the grandfather shook the boy's shoulders and then he released his firm grip and the young man stepped back.

"Yes, Grandpa," said the boy in an equally serious response, giving his shoulders a twist to ease out the pain.

"Didn't mean to hurt you, boy."

"That's okay."

The two sat back down on the porch's edge and they watched the sun slowly drop in the sky and with it the oppressing heat. A cooler breeze blew. In the late afternoon, across miles of open prairie land, they saw a wagon approach from the east. The two horses and the wheels of the wagon kicked up a trail of dust that rose and lingered for a long time in the dry air.

"Looks like your Pa coming back from town," commented the old man.

The gray haired oldster shaded his still sharp eyes while he peered off in the distance. He had always been proud of his keen sight. In the old days it had kept him alive from Indians, renegades, and from soldiers in the war.

"Pa told me to do my work and pay you no mind."

"You got your chores done, boy. Suppose you let me deal with your Dad."

"Then can I ask something, Grandpa?"

"You got time," answered the old man. "I reckon your Pa won't be here for awhile."

"What was it like to use a gun in those days and, and, well…"

"You're asking a mighty hard question, boy. If'n you weren't kin I'd take affront. You sit there and give me time to think on it."

Together the two sat in silence, aware of the descending sun. They peered off in the distance and studied the dust cloud made by the approaching wagon.

"First off, boy, pistols and rifles made this here west. They were as necessary as air and breathing. Without guns, none of us could have survived. It's not the way some of these greenhorns think now. Guns were necessary and that's a fact. No romanticizin or stretchin the truth on that."

The old man stood up and stared up at the darkening mountains; he turned back to the boy and scuffed a boot against the hard ground.

"Far as I'm concerned, right or wrong, our country was formed on clean living citizens having the right to bear arms, and that's the way it should be. It's what keeps our leaders in line and our country different from all those others. Without guns, there would'a been no settling of this territory, no western states, no peace. A man in those days had to protect himself, hunt game, and survive without law, and that's what we did."

The boy stared at his grandfather, listening intently.

"First man I ever kilt, I was fourteen years old. Two years older than you are now. I come back from huntin and Pa was lying dead in the cabin in Michigan, and the thief was standing over him with that drippin knife. I surprised that no good no account and when he came at me, I shot him. Then I buried Pa, took what was worth taking, and lit out for the west. Been here ever since, ceptin that time during the Great Rebellion."

"I'm listening, Grandpa."

Both were looking at the approaching dust cloud. It was now near six o'clock in the afternoon and the sun was well down in the cloudless blue sky.

"I joined up with some mountain men in St. Louis. I spent three winters with em, and it was from those men I learned all that I needed to know about survivin. It was a hard school and I became a man with the bark on. I told you some of them stories. Then I took up with the 49ers and hit a pocket of gold. I came back to St. Louis and that's where I met your Pa's mother. We married and for a while I settled on a ranch on the other side of the Mississippi. Are yeah listenin, boy?"

The lad nodded his head.

"That woman tried to change everything about me, and I just couldn't take no more and lit off again. But not before leaving her set up for life with everything I owned."

"Yes, Grandpa."

"Well, after that I lived with the Cheyenne for awhile. Years later, I scouted for wagon trains. Winters I spent in the shining mountains, and in the summers I traveled the plains and hunted buffalo. I went back to that ranch and visited and discovered I had a son, and that woman spent all the money on a big fancy house with all the trimmings. She latched on to me, and demanded I provide more. I did some. From the time I came back to visit, the war come along and I served in that, wasteful and terrible thing that was. I told ya some of them stories, too."

They could both see that the wagon had advanced much closer now.

"Men I kilt and things I done were living the life of a westerner. I was one of the first out here and nothing made more sense to me than breathing clean fresh air and having miles of open country twixt me and other men."

"Didn't you miss people, Grandpa?"

"From time to time I did, but going back amongst em cured me of that right quick."

"But what about Pa? Didn't you care about him?"

"I did, son, I did. When he was your age, and again when he turned fourteen, and sixteen, I came back to take him with me. By then it was too late. Seemed that his mother took all the fire and lust for adventure out of that boy."

The old man stood up and paced back and forth as he spoke.

"He wouldn't go with me, or have nothin to do with me, despite me providin money each year to his ma. That woman seemed to have a knack for spendin and I'm afraid not much went to your Pa. You can tell by what you got now. And, I gave his mother two fortunes."

"Pa sure is angry at you, Grandpa."

"That he is, boy. That he is."

The dust of the wagon was close now, and they both sat on the porch and watched it advance to the barn. It disappeared inside, and in the time it took to unharness the horses, the two talked quietly.

"Grandpa, when you going to have a chance to tell me the rest?"

"I ain't dead yet, boy. God gave me a strong body and we still got time."

"I'm afraid Pa won't let you stay here much longer."

"You got that right, son," called the boy's father as he came from around the back of the barn and approached the house quietly. "I wondered what the two of you were talking about and I wanted to give a listen. Old man, you're giving my son wrong notions and I want you out of here."

"This boy's my grandson, and I got a lot to teach and tell him about. Even if you don't like it."

"Old man, there's nothing you have to say that I want to have him hear. All you ever were is a no account with big windies to tell."

"You still believe that, son?"

"Don't you call me son! You never were no father to me, and you don't have any right!"

"Your mother sure got you in a knot, boy. She took and took and never gave—not to me, not to you, not to anybody. Despite what you think, I supported the two of you, and all she ever taught you were lies and hate."

"Don't you speak to me of my mother! You abandoned us! You get out of here, and don't you be telling lies to my son!"

"Lies? Lies? I never lied to no man! Even if you don't care to know nothin about me, my grandson does. We're family, blood kin, and as long as he's interested, he has a right to know about his grandpappy."

"Family? What do you know about that? All you ever

cared about was yourself."

"Not true, boy. I came back for you. The first time when you were this boy's age and you refused to go. Seems like your mother sucked all the life right out of you afore you ever got the chance to live it."

"You call wandering a life? I'm teaching this boy values, not silly dreams and exaggerated stories about some wild adventures."

"Your ma really got you twisted. I feel sorry for you. All you know is how to be bitter and mean. Your mother spent all that money on herself, while she bad mouthed me to you, and left you with nothing."

"I told you! You have no right to talk about my mother! I want you out of here old man."

"Alright son, I'll leave, but not before showing you and that grandson of mine somethin."

The old man turned to the boy.

"Boy, go get me my bags from the spare bedroom and bring em back to me."

In the boy's absence, the old man kept talking.

"You never believed I did all those things I tried to tell you about, did yeah?"

"No! Never!"

The boy returned with a leather saddlebag and handed it to his grandfather. The old man set it on the porch and rummaged a hand down one side and came out with a worn leather belt, holster, and an old pistol. This he unwrapped, placed around his waist and buckled it on. The pistol and holster rested high up on the right hip. He turned to the boy.

"Grandson, suppose you pick up two rocks. No, not the small ones, although there was a time I could hit those. You get two fist sized ones. Now stand off to my right and then throw one up and then the other. Be sure to toss it up and away from you."

"Old man!" shouted the angry father. "Don't you endanger my son with your foolishness!"

"Go ahead boy. Throw one and then the other as fast and high up as you can."

The lad complied. First went up one rock and then the other, in a high arc out in front of the three standing in the open yard. The old man drew the pistol and fired two quick shots. Both descending rocks were hit dead center and exploded in fragments.

"There's not ten living men in all the west that can do that there shootin," commented the old man reholstering his pistol. "I doubt if there's even that many. If'n you were to put up a target, I could put all six shots in it. If'n I loaded six shots."

The white haired man drew the pistol out again and ejecting two shells he took two more from loops in the belt and reloaded the pistol.

"This here revolver is a converted cap and ball .38. I carried this ever since I picked it up in the war."

Faster than either the bitter father or excited boy could see, the old man suddenly crouched and fanning the pistol, shot continuous roaring blasts into a corral post thirty feet away. Pieces of the top of the post splintered and flew with each shot.

"Nope, not five living people in all the west can shoot

like that. And son, that's only part of what I learned in my life."

"That only proves what a ridiculous life you lived, father. Who cares if you can shoot?"

"It's proof, son, proof that all I say is the truth. Grandson, I'm leavin now. But I'll be back in a couple years. When I do, you decide whether you want to stay on this rock farm or go with me."

"Yes, Grandpa," answered the boy excitedly. "I'll be ready."

"Father! Don't you never come back here! You're not taking my boy from me!"

"You had your chance," answered the wiry old man. "Years ago I asked you three times to go with me, and you chose to stay with your ma. Look at all the good that did."

"She taught me the value of hard work and to stick with something I started. That's more than can be said about you! I won't never abandon my son."

"No, you'd stay here and work him to death while stealing his dreams and his heritage. Something I tried to give to you and you refused."

"What heritage?"

"A life of freedom, a life of exploration, and travel. The buffalo are gone now, and the Indians put down, but there's still mountains to explore, streams to fish, animals to hunt, and land to see."

"A life of idleness and waste!"

"Where do you think all that money came from that your mother spent? It was out there, and I still know where some of it is. That's only part of the legacy I can teach this boy."

The angry father stared at the old man without answer. The grandfather ejected the empty shells on the ground and reloaded the pistol. Picking up the saddlebags, the oldster whistled and an ugly gray mustang gelding came to the front gate of the corral. Removing tack from the fence rail, the old man bridled and saddled the horse, and tied down the saddle bags. Mounting spryly, he spoke to the two standing in the yard, while adjusting his wide sombrero on his gray haired head.

"Son, this land was made for buffalo, and later for horses and cows. It ain't meant to be plowed up and farmed, exceptin for small gardens. Continue this hard rock ranch, and it'll send you to an early grave."

"Now you're telling me how to live?"

"Don't let your bitterness fall on this boy. He has a right to what his granddad can teach him. When I come back, you let him go."

The gray jumped to a trot and then into a running gallop as the old man leaned forward to give the horse more speed. Father and son stood in the yard and watched the retreating form. The trailing dust cloud of horse and man lingered for some time before it disappeared behind a descending hill.

*1st Printing, *THE SHOOTEST,* May/June 2007

GRANDMA GIVES NO QUARTER

Frances Stevens' steady hand did not betray her eighty-two years as she stood in the kitchen ladling soup into a bowl for her daughter-in-law. The two women talked lightly about chores that had to be completed and food to be preserved before Frances's son, Charles, and his cowhands returned from a small cattle drive to Abilene. Except for old Stumpy, the cook, and George and Sam, the two old-timers who cared for the stock, the ranch was devoid of hands.

Ever since Whitey Stevens died of old age and hard work, Grandma Frances helped run the ranch with an iron hand and she knew how to handle the shotgun hidden behind the curtained kitchen pantry. Grandma may have years on her side, but her resolve and spirit was as young as ever. So, it was no surprise to her, with her lifetime of experience in the hard west, to see outriders come galloping up to the house, six-guns thundering.

As the shots rang across the yard, old George rushed out of the barn, pitchfork in hand and mouth open. Sam was standing at the water trough. Neither stablemen were armed so they made no threatening move. The outriders were dressed in ragged and dirty military clothing. The only things gleaming and shining in the noonday sun were the oiled leather holsters, pistols, and the rifles they carried.

Stumpy looked out the window of the cook shack attached to the large bunkhouse way down by the creek. He didn't give himself away but looked closely to see that the riders were riffraff from the war between the rebs and yanks, and they were experienced killers. The old man counted five heavily armed men. He limped with his wooden leg across to his private quarters in a cramped room behind the cookhouse. Off the wall he took a double-barreled shotgun and from a bag he took several handfuls of double aught buckshot and began stuffing his pockets.

"If those men come down here, at least some of em will not survive the trip," Stumpy mumbled under his breath as he placed the bag back on the nail.

* * *

"I'll handle this, Abigail," said Grandma Stevens. "You just calm yourself and start the large pot and make all the coffee you can put to boil."

She walked calmly to the kitchen door, opened it, and stepped out onto the side porch.

"You men make a noisy entrance. If you're hungry light down and I'll feed you."

"Why that's right neighborly of you, Grandma," said the one who appeared to be the leader.

The man dismounted and his men followed suit. All of them looked carefully around. The leader whistled loudly and from up the road came riding two more men, one young and the other with long gray hair and wearing a black patch over one eye. Both held rifles in their right hands. The two rode up, dismounted, and stood next to their horses.

"Jack and Sonny," said the leader. "We're going in for dinner. Tie these two old timers up and put them on the porch. Jack, you go check the outbuildings and make sure no one else is about. Sonny, you water the horses. Find hay and toss it down right here to feed em."

As the two latecomers left to do as ordered, the five other men made their way into the kitchen and took seats around a large table. Grandma went into the curtained pantry and brought out air tights of beans and set them on the dry sink. She went back for a haunch of bacon wrapped in cheesecloth and dropped it heavily next to the beans. Lifting down two large iron skillets from hooks on the wall, she set them on the end of the dry sink. She opened the air tights and poured beans into one pan and cut up the bacon and laid the large, thin pieces into the other.

The five dirty and smelly men talked loudly and made rude and bold comments concerning the good looks of the younger woman. Hearing enough, Grandma Stevens turned. She held the large butcher knife in her hand and pointed to all the men.

"Mind your manners. This is my kitchen and you hold your piece. Show some respect or pay the consequences."

The men stopped their jeering and looked at the stern speaking white haired woman. They began to guffaw.

"Grandma," said the leader in amusement. "What are you going to do, slice all of us with that butcher knife, or are you gonna poison us?"

"Not a bad idea, sonny. Now you do what your mommas taught you—if any of you men can remember—and mind your manners. This is a decent house and you men will act decent."

The five foul-smelling men were silent for a moment. Suddenly two removed their hats with flourishing sweeps revealing long, greasy, and unkempt hair. All of them burst out in loud whoops. Several thumped their fists on the wooden table in grand amusement. Abigail Stevens, her face ashen, was already building up the fire in the cook stove to heat the frying pans of food. The coffee boiled. While the outlaws waited for their meal, they told rude and ribald jokes. Abigail went for cups. On her way back toward the table she caught the warning shake of Grandma's head. Abigail walked over to the dry sink.

"I'll serve the men, you cook the food," said Grandma.

Grandma Frances took five cups, set them on the table, then went to the stove where her daughter-in-law stood stirring beans and bacon. Grandma took the smaller enameled coffee pot, returned to the table, and poured all the coffee that was in it. She managed to fill four cups. Returning to the stove she placed a towel on the handle of the larger coffee pot and carried it to the table. She filled the last cup, and set the large pot on a metal trivet.

"Good coffee, Grandma," commented the outlaw leader. "Think you can take a couple of cups out for Jack and Sonny?"

The gray haired woman took down two cups and poured coffee into them. Carrying them by their handles she gently shoved the screen door open and walked out onto the wide porch that surrounded one side of the ranch house. She went down the steps and up to the young man. Sonny was breaking up a bale of hay and tossing bunches on the ground in front of the horses tied to the rail. Grandma Frances noted that the bits were pulled from their mouths so they could chew. She eyed the young man and realized that he was not like the others. He wore fresh clothing and was clean-shaven.

"Here's some coffee," she said softly. "What is a decent looking lad like you doing with this group of murderers?"

Sonny, startled by the woman's presence, turned abruptly, stood erect, and took one of the cups.

"Ma'am? Thank you, ma'am."

"My name is Grandma Stevens."

"Excuse me, Grandma? You asked me a question?"

"I asked what a nice looking young man like you is doing with this bunch of cutthroats?"

"Well, ma'am, uh, Grandma Stevens. My pa died. These men came to our ranch while I was burying him and took all the food and everything not tied down. They just sort of dragged me along and put me to work handling the horses."

"Is that agreeable with you?"

"No, ma'am. It ain't."

"Are they as bad as they look?"

"Oh, yes. There ain't one thing they wouldn't do. They've killed and stolen all the way across Kansas and into Colorado."

"Here comes that Jack. Give him this cup of coffee. Tell

him I'll bring dinner shortly. Are you willing to join us?"

"Doing what, Grandma?"

"You follow my lead, Sonny. If I can't get them to leave peaceable, will you back me with that six-gun of yours?"

"It's too dangerous," protested the youth. "They'll kill all of you!"

"You just pay attention and let me worry about that. I'll ask you once again, will you join us in a pinch?"

Sonny stared into the bright blue eyes of the gray haired woman.

"Yes, Grandma," he finally answered.

"Good."

"Say there," growled One-Eyed Jack. "What're you two whispering about?"

"I was telling Sonny here, that dinner would be brought out shortly. He has your coffee."

The old woman boldly walked up the steps and opened the screen door to the kitchen. She hurried to the stove where her terrified daughter-in-law was ladling beans and bacon onto stone plates. She gave the younger woman's arm a reassuring squeeze. Grandma piled a plate high with thick slices of bread and placed it on the table beside a tub of sweet butter. Then she served the men their meals. Putting bread on two extra plates, and taking two forks, Grandma took the food out through the kitchen and onto the porch. Jack pushed Sonny aside in his hurry to grab a plate. Grandma held on firmly to the last dish, handed it to the boy, smiled, and winked.

Grandma Stevens went back into the kitchen, walked around the long table and watched the men devour their food. Using the bread, they mopped up the last of the beans and the bacon grease. All five of them were bent over their plates making slurping noises.

"Is there something you want, Grandma?" growled the leader as his eyes met her stare.

"Yes. What's your name?"

"Jake," answered the outlaw.

"Jake what?"

"Grandma, you try my patience. Jake is the only name I'm giving out."

"Well, Jake, I have an offer to make you and your men."

The others stopped eating and looked up in open curiosity.

"What kind of offer?"

"A better one than you'll get anywhere else. The war is over and has been for four years. The country's changing, and people and the law won't tolerate takers."

"Now, Grandma, I'd kill a man for standing there and saying that to me," said Jake. "Be careful what more you say."

"I'll give you an opportunity to leave here in peace without the law having to look for you."

"What do you have on your mind, old woman? I'll remind you before you start to fib us, that one of your good neighbors told us your men are on a cattle drive to Abilene. Not expected back for weeks. We already know we can pretty well do as we please here for quite a while."

"I figured."

"Well, go on, what's this big offer you want to make us?"

"In exchange for leaving the ranch and my daughter-in-law alone, we'll cook for you and wait on you until you're ready to leave."

"That's not much of an offer, Grandma."

"Hear me out. In that cookie jar up on that cabinet over there is one hundred and eighty dollars. Back at the cook shack is a month's supply of flower, bacon, rice, and air tights. In the bunkhouse are extra range clothing, boots, hats, Sunday-go-to-meeting suits, underwear, socks, and a big tin bathing tub. We could heat water for you, and each of you men could have a good bath with lye soap and throw out those awful clothes you're wearing. Heaven knows you sure smell ripe. You could re-supply what you need. We'll butcher a yearling steer, cook potatoes, take greens from the gardens, and cook for you until you decide to go. How about it?"

"Lady, we can already do that without your help."

"You telling me that any of your men can cook like I can?"

"She sure got that right!" yelled one of the outlaws.

"You leave here on peaceable terms and I won't call the law," Grandma offered.

"Grandma!" said Jake thumping the table hard and his dark eyes flashing. "You trying to put something slick past me? We like taken' what we want—besides, the boys and I plan to have a little fun with that daughter-in-law of yours. Right boys?"

The four men hoo-rawed followed by a shout from One-Eyed Jack listening in from the porch.

"See, Grandma! We take what we want, and nothing

ever stops us."

"Is that your final answer?" asked the gray haired woman.

"For now it is. But second thought, I like that part you said about the boys getting a bath and some clean clothes. They are ripe and I can't even stand myself downwind. Old lady, you and your daughter-in-law get that tub and heater up. We'll take turns taking a bath. Me first!"

The men laughed and hooted again.

"Don't you get no ideas, old woman. We're good at re-supplying, but we could use some down home cooking. Jack!" called the leader through the screen door. "You untie those two old men and get them to catching and butchering a steer. We'll fill up on beef tonight, compliments of our two lady cooks!"

The men cheered again, this time much louder. One of them jumped up, grabbed the terrified Abigail, and swung her around in a circle. He bent to give her a kiss and Grandma Stevens thumped him on the head with a wooden ladling spoon. The man dropped Abigail and reached for his pistol. The leader's arm shot up and blocked the gunman.

"Not yet, Zeb. Not til I say so," he ordered.

Again the men in the kitchen began to laugh and point at the angry killer—the loudest of them all was the leader Jake.

"So long as you want us to wait on you," said Grandma Stevens angrily, "you men will behave yourselves."

"Well!" shouted Jake still laughing. "You heard her, boys!"

With this momentary truce, Grandma shoved Abigail through the screen door and they hurried to the cook shack. They entered the small building and Grandma called out in a loud whisper.

"Stumpy? Stumpy, are you in here?"

A muffled voice answered and from the back bedroom Stumpy showed his face.

"I'm here."

"No time to talk. These men plan to do us harm. I want you to hide and be ready with that shotgun of yours."

"How will I know when it's time?"

"Stumpy, we're going to take the tin tub and carry it over to the porch. We'll heat water and the leader is going to take a bath. You watch out, the men will be looking around for clothing in here. I suggest you get outside the back door, sneak around the side of the house, and hide in the bushes. But first, give me some of that poison you got."

"What poison?"

"Stumpy, don't fool with me. The poison you give the cowboys when they act up. I need something to put in the coffee and make these men sick, and I mean in a hurry."

The cook limped on his peg leg over to a cabinet. He opened a drawer and took out a bottle wrapped in a brown cloth. He removed the cloth and handed the bottle with the dark liquid to the woman.

"Put this in the coffee. Two drops will make them darn sick. Use the whole thing and within five minutes they'll be doubled over in pain and hardly be able to move."

"Thanks, Stumpy. One last thing, don't hurt the boy

with that gang; he's on our side. Now get going!"

Grandma motioned Abigail into the next room where standing against the far wall was the tub. They both picked it up and wrestled with it to the front door. As they were struggling, two of the gunmen came in through the cook shack.

"Say, what's taking so long?" asked one of the men suspiciously.

"I'm too old to get the tub through this door," answered Grandma. "Suppose you help us?"

The rough garbed men came over and took the place of the women. They lifted and turned the tub and managed to get it out the door.

"Where do you want it?"

"On the porch," answered Grandma. "Next to the kitchen. That way we can fill it with hot water."

The outlaws carried the metal tub across the yard and placed it where the gray haired woman pointed. Then Abigail and Grandma turned to go back up the steps of the porch and into the kitchen. On the way, Grandma Frances went near Sonny who was currying one of the horses.

"Sonny," she whispered. "Whatever you do, don't drink any more coffee!"

Grandma put more wood in the huge iron cookstove and stoked the fire. Abigail filled pots and pans with water from the kitchen pump and placed them on the cook plates. The two women pumped cold water into buckets which they carried to the porch and poured into the tub. To this they would add the hot water. Grandma picked up the large empty coffee pot from the table and filled it with water. She took down more coffee beans and ground them with the grinder fastened to the end of the dry sink. Removing the little brown bottle from her apron pocket, she pulled out the cork. As she added coffee to the large pot, she turned over the bottle, and dumped the brown liquid in. She closed the lid and placed the coffee pot on the stove to boil.

Abigail was standing at the sink with a frightened expression on her face. Grandma gave her a stern look, took a deep breath, and then smiled at her daughter-in-law. Abigail understood and tried to relax. After several deep breaths, her look of terror lessoned. Grandma kept right on smiling.

All the men except One-Eye Jack, who now had entered the kitchen to watch the women, were in the bunkhouse picking out new clothes. Even from this distance, the men could be heard laughing and making loud comments over their newfound possessions.

"I want some coffee, woman!" growled Jack.

"It's boiling now," answered Grandma smoothly.

"Well, hurry up!"

"It'll be ready as soon as the men get back."

"Won't do no good. Then it'll be my turn to grab some duds. Don't know why they always make me last. Me and that boy always got to do the guarding. I don't get no respect."

"How about some cookies?" asked Grandma pleasantly.

"Don't mind if I do."

Grandma went in the pantry. While she was behind the curtain, she quickly pulled out the shotgun and took a coat off a hook on the wall. She placed the shotgun on a shelf in easy reach and put the coat over it. Then she brought out a tin with cookies. She opened it and set it on the table in front of the filthy one-eyed man. Jack grunted and turned over the tin and dumped all the cookies onto the wooden table. Greedily he began to bite into them, chewing two at a time and swallowing loudly.

"Ummm, good, would be better with coffee."

As the man ate, Grandma went over to the sink and picked up a small but sharp carving knife and put it into the pocket of her apron. She looked at Abigail. Clumsily, the young woman picked up a knife, and dropped it into her apron pocket. The two women then stood against the dry sink and watched and listened silently to the noises of the one eyed outlaw as he devoured the decreasing pile of cookies.

The gunmen began to return to the kitchen. With them they brought new clothing. One outlaw was carrying a brand new broadcloth suit; others had combinations of Sunday suit jackets, canvass pants, vests, boots, hats, underwear, and socks. The leader, Jake, brought back the best of the pick. Besides dress pants, he had new boots, shirt, hat, vest, and a leather coat. Disregarding the women, the leader began to strip in the kitchen and Grandma spoke up.

"Jake, have some coffee," she announced. "Then remove your clothing outside so we can pick it up and burn it."

All the men laughed crazily as Jake stopped undressing. He sat down and took the offered coffee. The other four men did the same. Grandma put the hot coffee pot on the iron grate on the table and then walked to the screen door. She watched as the one-eyed bandit and Sonny made their way to the bunkhouse to select clean clothing. It was obvious that Jack wasn't going to have a chance to drink the coffee. Grandma Stevens worried if the young man Sonny was up to what needed to be done.

Following Grandma's lead, Abigail began carrying the steaming pots of hot water outside and dumping them into the tin bathing tub. Jake went out, stripped, and got into the water. Grandma went back into the pantry and came out with a large cake of lye soap and a white towel. She handed the soap to the outlaw leader and he complained loudly.

"More hot water, Grandma! And bring me a scrub brush!"

Grandma went back in the pantry and brought out a brush and took it to the naked man. In her mind she began to count up to the five minutes—the time Stumpy said the poison would begin to take affect. It was very near that time now. Suddenly the outlaw leader convulsed in the tub full of water and violently grabbed at his stomach. The leader looked over at the gray haired woman. There was surprise and pain in the man's face.

"My stomach hurts!" gasped Jake.

There was another violent stab of pain and yet another and the outlaw doubled up in agony and water splashed.

"What did you do to me?" bellowed the angry man.

Jake reached out his right hand and grabbed the old woman by the sleeve of her dress. Savagely he pulled her across the tub and began to throttle her with both hands.

Grandma struggled and reached down and pulled the carving knife from her apron. With all her strength she plunged the point of the knife deep into the man's chest. Dark crimson flowed from the wound. As she let go of the knife, he slipped down into the water and it turned red. Grandma Stevens hurriedly made her way into the kitchen and to the pantry. Two of the outlaws raced past her and onto the porch. The men were doubled over and grabbing at their stomachs. It was the same for the two still sitting at the kitchen table.

There were loud shouts of "Murder" and "Kill them" from the two men on the porch. Outside a shotgun blasted and then fired again. There was the thump of falling bodies. The two men at the kitchen table arose from their seats, doubled over in pain, and reached for their guns. From the pantry emerged the old woman. In her hands was the double-barreled shotgun with both hammers pulled back. Abigail looked on in disbelief at the grim expression on Grandma's face as she pointed and pulled the trigger of one barrel. Abigail saw her mother-in-law kicked back by the awful blast of the .12 gauge and nearly fall. She recovered and aimed again. The double barreled shotgun blasted and blood again splattered across the kitchen wall. The two outlaws were nearly torn in two as they flew back from the power of each discharge. Grandma, for a second time was thrust backwards and this time she lost her balance and fell.

Abigail ran to her mother-in-law's side and noted that the older woman had hit her head. Blood was flowing from underneath her hair and pooling on the floor. Abigail grabbed a towel from the counter, bunched it, and pressed it against the wound.

"Grandma!" she said. "Talk to me!"

"Daughter," whispered Grandma. "What about the bunkhouse?"

Both stared at each other, there was a pistol shot, and then another.

"Help me to my feet, daughter. We have to reload the shotgun. If the boy hasn't got that one-eyed monster, we're going to be in a whole heap of trouble."

Too late, they heard footsteps. Both women turned their eyes and there stood the young man, pistol in hand.

"Grandma," called the lad. "Your plan worked."

Both women sighed in relief. They heard running footsteps followed by the entrance of George and Sam. Then came the steady thump of wood on wood and eventually Stumpy was at the door holding his shotgun.

"Well," he said. "Don't want to do that again."

"What I want to know," asked old George. "Who's going to explain this to the boss?"

"For now," said Grandma Stevens sternly. "That would be me, and the only explaining needed to be done is to the sheriff."

*1st Printing, *ROPE AND WIRE,* July 2008

HOT DESERT, HOT ROCK, HOT SNAKE

The sun shone down through the large blue dome of the cloudless sky. It was the height of summer. The air was stifling and all creatures, both man and beast, suffered to breathe—all except the reptilians. The rattlesnake crawled out into the open and propelled its long undulating body across the desert floor. It came to a jumble of rocks and slithered higher, forcing its way on its rippling belly. It found a flat spot. There it coiled and sunned itself in the intense heat. It looked with its dark beady eyes and froze, not moving, except for the tongue which darted in, out, in, and out. Its multi-hued body matched the rock perfectly and the snake was almost invisible.

The rider on the sweating horse came up the trail. The horse was thirsty and tired, and so was the rider. They longed for cool shade and the relief of water, but that was miles and miles away across the prairie and near the foothills. They climbed higher and there was a fifty foot drop onto rocks, cactus, piñon, and cedar trees below. The tired horse stumbled and nearly fell and the rider pulled up on the reins.

"Fool horse!" said the man. "You want to kill us both?"

In the intense heat, the horse hesitated, snorted, and continued on. Man and beast sweated heavily, and breathing came hard to both of them. The dry air sucked the moisture from their bodies, and the sweat evaporated leaving no cool effect. The mouth and lips dried too, and in the hot air it was difficult to swallow. They must reach water and shade, or suffer more—perhaps even die.

The canteens the man carried in this high desert were empty. Because of the drought, the last water hole was dry. The man counted on that spring. Now he was forced to travel without a supply of water. Ordinarily the man would have wet a rag and swabbed out the dusty nostrils of the horse. They would have paused to drink a small portion of water. Now they had none, and they must continue on in this terrible heat.

The snake first felt the vibration of horse hooves through its body long before it saw man and animal coming toward it. The weak eyes saw a blob of black approaching. Its tongue tasted the sweat of the two creatures. The closer they came the more the rattler sensed the heat of the large bodies. The reptile had just molted and the rattles were noiseless. Its tail would give no warning. If they came too close it would strike out in defense. The snake lay unmoving, waiting, and watching.

Normally the horse would have smelled or sensed the snake, as it too was susceptible to its bite. But the animal was tired, its nose caked with dust, and its keen senses dulled. The steed plodded tiredly along, wishing for shade, rest, and water. When horse and man came to the large flat rock at knee level, the snake struck out, and propelled three quarters of its body forward. Almost faster than the eyes could see, its sharp fangs sunk into the exposed thigh of the man. The rider gave a high pitched yell, and the startled beast, seeing the snake and hearing the sudden noise of the man, bucked and leaped away.

Thrown out of the saddle, the rider landed in stunning force on the rock ledge where the snake lay. Before the man could move the snake struck again and yet another time, and then slithered off the rock. The second bite made two fang marks in the cheek, the third went deep into the neck, next to the jugular vein. There was little movement by the man except for him to realize he was seriously hurt, and that the snake had bitten him again.

The mustang ran up the trail and stopped. From a distance, the horse saw the snake slither down the rock and disappear. Gradually, the four-legged animal came close to sniff at its owner. It stayed loyal to the man as long as he continued to breathe. When no sign of life showed, the saddled mustang turned and went up the trail.

In the dark crack of a rock, the rattlesnake lay. Its sensitive body now telling it that the danger of the living creatures had passed. After a time, it came back out into the light of day. It found another flat rock to slither onto and again it luxuriated in the heat of the sun.

HARD TIMES FOR BILLY O'REILLY

Billy got up from his rag bed in the alley and knew he was in trouble. The group of orphans he had tangled with the night before were gathered in a bunch in front of him and all had sneering grimaces on their dirty faces. Several held clubs or pieces of brick. These boys wouldn't tolerate a newcomer to their territory, and yesterday they had chased him when he stole an apple from the outdoor stand. One of them got too close and Billy slugged him. Now that boy stood in front of his gang slapping a club against his left hand.

"We don't have no room on our block for new blokes," called out the leader. "Shortly you won't be breathin. Sides, I owe you for that bash in the face."

Billy wasn't green to Irish Town, but he was new to being an orphan, and pressed by hunger, he had wandered off from his own city blocks. Typhoid took his folks, and now he was as homeless as these lads before him. He wasn't going to fight all of them and live, running was his only chance. There was a fence behind him, and being wiry and skinny, Billy turned, ran for it, and scrambled up the wooden barrier, climbed over, and jumped down.

Behind him came the angry calls of the mob of boys, quickly followed by a bombardment of stones, bricks, and sticks.

Placing a forearm across his face, Billy ran. A wooden stick flew, hit his arm and it stung. He dodged the bricks and kept running, putting distance between himself and the screaming mob. The leader climbed up the fence and gave a high pitched whistle. More gang members appeared and joined the chase. Billy turned and saw boys scale the fence, jump down, and race towards him.

Billy continued to run. He came to a busy street and turned right along a large brick building. He had no advantage here. He didn't know these boys or the neighborhood. If he got away, he would be very lucky. Billy ran as fast as he could and, seeing a wagon with its tailgate down, he jumped aboard and hid behind some barrels. Several of the gang turned the corner and saw him. They screamed out Billy's location. When the wagon turned another corner, Billy jumped out and ran down an alley. Gasping and trying to catch his breath, he hid behind a pile of trash.

New York was full of homeless boys and they were a tough bunch. They had to be to avoid the coppers. They survived by stealing and using their numbers to prey on folks. The police were tough on them, and if caught, they would be beaten and sent to an alms or work house.

Fourteen-year-old Billy knew he was in a fix. He heard the mob signaling back and forth to each other.

"He's over here! Let's get him!"

Billy heard voices coming towards him. He jumped up

and ran to the end of the alley and found a narrow opening between two buildings. He turned sideways and began to squeeze through the crevice; his clothes caught and tore on the rough bricks as he moved. Only the smaller boys would be able to follow him here. The narrow tunnel between the brick buildings finally ended. He emerged covered with coal dust. Turning the corner at full speed, he slammed into the chest of a uniformed copper, nearly knocking him over. The angry officer lashed out repeatedly with his club. Billy fell unconscious.

The policeman called for assistance by blowing his whistle. The boy was hit hard and did not come to. Not even as two officers dragged him unconscious through the streets to their precinct house.

"What you got there?" shouted the sergeant behind the desk.

"A filthy, thieving orphan, that's what!" answered the corporal to the sergeant. "The little beggar came right at me, he did. He nearly knocked me down! After my change purse, I bet. I arrest him for attackin and assaultin an officer of the law!"

"Well, what's his name?"

"Haw, haw, haw," laughed the other officer. "Hank here hit him upside the head and the lad ain't talkin just yet!"

The three officers laughed.

"Throw him in the holding tank with the drunks," ordered the sergeant. "All the other cells are full of these rascals. Any more, and we'll have to ship em out."

"That'd save the city some pennies," growled the arresting officer. "Put em all on a train and let them westerners teach them a thing or two."

The men laughed as two of them dragged the unconscious boy to the lock up.

Awareness came slowly to Billy. He came to the edge of consciousness several times, heard mumbled voices, and then the pain was too much. He fell back into blackness. Eventually he awoke to a pulsing in his head. The injury was bad, and it was agony for him to breathe. Lying there, he tried to remember who he was and what was happening to him. He began to remember his mother's face and softly called out to her. There was laughter, and he opened his eyes.

He was in a jail cell and there were filthy men and boys crowded around him. Dozens of eyes stared.

"He called out to his mommy!" declared a brutal looking man.

Again there was desultory laughter.

Billy slowly sat up and felt the back of his neck. There was a laceration and it hurt. He drew his hand away and it was covered with wet and crusted blood. Billy still didn't know who he was or why he was there. The pain of his bruises, and the back of his head made it hard to think. Then all of a sudden it came back with a rush. He was Billy O'Reilly. His parents died of the typhoid and he was homeless. It was a copper who hit him.

"Where, where am I?" asked the youth.

"Well, it ain't home," answered the tough sarcastically.

Again, there was scattered laughter. Billy looked up at the man and then around at the others. All wore dirty and ragged clothing. Billy tried to stand up, then fainted. His body folded and his forehead came down hard against the cement floor. Skin split and there was more blood. This time, no one in the crowded cell laughed.

"Hey!" yelled a boy to the guards. "There's someone hurt in here! He needs help!"

"Stop your yelling!" responded the tough man. "You'll get us a beatin! They ain't going to help no orphan, and we'll all be lucky if we get fed. Nearly every day they haul a dead body out of here. If you want to help the waif, then fix him yourself!"

The lad who spoke did as suggested. He slid off the bench and knelt beside the unconscious boy. After examining his neck, he pulled up the boy's shirt tails and began to tear off strips. Some of the cloth he folded and applied to the oozing laceration. He tied another strip tightly around the neck to hold the bandage in place, but not tight enough to stop his breathing. Turning the boy over, he did the same with the cut on his forehead.

"Good job!" commented the tough man. "Now he can die all fixed up."

Several officers came in with a big soup kettle. They ladled gruel into bowls and handed it through the bars. Men and boys alike fought to be first. The guards yelled and cursed as they tried to serve the slop.

"Filthy bunch of animals!" yelled one of the guards. "Get back, or none of yeah will git nothing!"

The boy who had helped Billy got a bowl and downed the watery substance. It was tasteless and bland. He handed the dish back. In the confusion he managed to get a second bowl. He rushed back to the injured lad and shook him.

Billy groaned and opened his eyes.

"Listen to me. You better eat this, don't know when they'll feed us again."

He raised the bowl to Billy's lips, forced his mouth open, and poured the gray contents in. Much of it ended up on the floor.

"What you helping him for?" asked the tough man. "You're wasting good food."

"Give me that bowl back!" shouted a guard. "Or yeah don't get fed next time!"

Hurriedly the tough man grabbed the bowl and shoved it through the bars.

This went on for several days and eventually Billy got better. He learned his friend's name was Kelly and his parents, too, had died from typhoid. Their stories were similar.

The crowded cells began to smell worse, and so did those who occupied them. When the prisoners thought they could take it no longer, officials came and separated the youth from the adults. Some of the men wore clerical clothes. The administrators decided who would go to orphanages, almshouses, or be assigned work. Kelly and Billy tried to stick together but were separated. Billy never knew what happened to the Irish boy who had saved his life.

Billy was asked many questions by three men wearing religious clothing. At the end of the interview he heard the phrase "place him out." He was marched to a warehouse with other boys. Remaining in line, they were led to large tubs and ordered to bathe. Using lye soap, Billy scrubbed his hair and body, and felt much cleaner. His dirty clothes were discarded and replaced with a man sized outfit.

Once clean, the boys were fed a meager meal. That night, Billy and the others were locked in the warehouse. The next morning they were marched through town to the train station and herded onto the platform. Billy saw girls and young children put on separate cars. He guessed this must be an orphan train. He asked an escort what it was all about, and was told to hold his tongue and mind his manners.

Perhaps, thought Billy. *It will be better to go west. There will be cowboys and Indians, buffalo, and wide open spaces*.

That's all he really knew about it. For certain, anything was better than that jail cell and the dirty cold streets of the city.

They traveled day and night and were fed bread, cheese, and apples. Billy was surprised to see so much green and so many gardens, houses, and farms. The further west they went, the more open the sky. The clear air made the distances greater. This land was vast, so empty and lonely looking. Billy forced himself to stay awake. From dawn to dusk he looked out the windows, not wanting to miss any of the views.

The train began to make stops, and groups of children were unloaded. They disappeared into churches, courthouses, and other large buildings. Then the orphan train started up again. It was when they passed over the Mississippi River into Kansas that the sky really opened up. It was a great dome of blue with the piercing light of the sun shining over prairie grass that stretched for a hundred miles. The vision of open plains was more than his mind could absorb.

What type of people lived in such country? wondered Billy.

Billy's group was the first to board and the last to leave. The train stopped at a small village in Kansas. The children were unloaded and taken to a little white church at the end of town. Young couples, along with single men and women were waiting. The rugged westerners filed into the church and examined the children lined up in front of them. It was obvious all these folk had come to pick out those they wished to take home.

The younger children were picked first. A small boy and girl were chosen by a kind looking couple who smiled as they took hold of little hands. Billy was the oldest and the last to be chosen. A man in a leather apron approached him. His face was burned dark by the western sun. He was short and wiry and he smelled of smoke. His bare sinewy forearm and bicep bulged as he pointed and spoke about Billy.

"This the last of the group?" asked the blacksmith pointing at the boy and talking to one of the train escorts.

"Yes sir."

"Well, tarnation! He's a skinny pup. I wanted a boy that could pay his way."

"Sir, our charity, The New York Juvenile Asylum, asks you to take in this youngster and love him and provide him a good home. Not to work…"

"Seems to me you city folk don't have much charity

sending your orphans out here. You should be lucky I'm even considering the scrawny thing."

"Sir, he's a poor unfortunate who deserves…"

"You want him?" snarled the blacksmith. "Then take him!"

"Sir! Good gracious! His name is Billy O'Reilly. He's a good…"

"Irish! No decent folk would want him!"

"He's just a…"

"Hush, if you're going to leave him, bring em down to my shop. But mind you, feed him first, cause I want him workin' the minute you drop him off."

Billy knew by the look on the train escort's face that he was going to take him down to that man's shop. The escort led him to a little restaurant on the dusty street and ordered chicken and potatoes. The charity man kept apologizing to Billy. The boy hungrily devoured all the food as quickly as he could. He had learned to eat during adversity, knowing full well the next meal might not come at all.

"I'm sorry, lad," said the charity man. "You're the last, and I can't take you back with me. I hope you enjoyed the meal, son. I paid for it myself."

With that, Billy was taken to the blacksmith's shop. They found it easily by the rising smoke and the ringing of a hammer on hot iron.

Billy O'Reilly's life became a nightmare. From sun-up to dark he labored for the blacksmith. The old man was called Smitty by the residents of the town, but he demanded that Billy call him MISTER Smitty. There wasn't one moment of the day that the mean old blacksmith didn't complain.

"You skinny, worthless, good for nothin, you're eating me out of house and home. You Irish, you're nothing but a bunch of potato mashers, running all over the country taking jobs."

"You chose ME, Mister," responded Billy angrily. "It's the only reason I'm here."

It became Billy's task to fix breakfast, lunch, and supper. There were always potatoes or beans with the meals, but no other greens. Taking it upon himself, by lantern light, Billy turned up the soil behind the shop and planted vegetables. Billy had a hankering for carrots, peas, and lettuce, and carefully he weeded, nurtured and watered his garden. He added these meager gatherings into the meals he was forced to fix. With the nutritious food and hard work Billy began to fill out and grow.

Smitty, a hard man, also drank. When he was drunk he beat the boy. At these times Billy tried his best to stay out of the old man's way. When Smitty was hung over, work stopped and customers complained. For this reason Smitty taught his helper how to hammer and form hot iron into useful items. Their most pressing trade was farrier work. Billy became an expert at making and shoeing horses and the business profited.

It was a hard life, and winter and summer Billy slept on a cot at the back of the shop. In the winter, the nights were cold. Without permission Billy built a room around his bed, and made a little stove and chimney to keep warm. Smitty complained, beat the boy, but left the room standing.

There were people in town who felt sorry for Billy, but

minded their own business. The smithy was tough and not even the town marshal would confront this ornery old miser.

Four years later, dressed in rags and hand-me-downs, eighteen-year-old Billy challenged Smitty for wages.

"What?" screamed the man pointing at him. "You don't even pay for the food and shelter I provide!"

"Not true, Smitty!" answered the boy.

It was the middle of a hot Saturday summer afternoon and a crowd was on the streets. They stopped to listen. It was by no accident Billy had chosen this time.

"It's MISTER Smitty to you, boy!"

"Not any more, old man. Ever since I came here, you've yelled, shouted, complained, beat me, and treated me like a slave. Those days are over!"

"Shut up, boy!" responded Smitty, nervously looking at the crowd and then at Billy. "Get back to work or I'll knock some sense into ya."

"Not this time, Smitty!"

The blacksmith was still a tough muscled old man, but heavy drink had taken a lot out of him. Smitty came at the boy with a four pound hammer in his hand and swung it. Billy, wiry and fast, easily stepped out of the way.

"Why you!" shouted Smitty.

The town marshal heard the commotion and came running over. He pushed through the crowd and watched as the youth and the blacksmith finally had it out. There was no doubt who the onlookers favored. It was sympathy for the young man that kept anyone from interfering.

The short old man had a lifetime of thick muscle on

him. Billy was tall and wiry. Through swinging a heavy hammer and shoeing unruly mustangs he had developed wide shoulders and bulging biceps. The old man attacked again with the four pounder and Billy dodged. One time the young man tripped and Smitty thumped him hard in the chest. The crowd groaned. Billy grabbed Smitty's wrists and they rolled around in the dirt, testing each other's strength. The old man broke Billy's hold and began to throttle the youth's throat.

Grasping the man's wrists again, Billy rose to his feet. He lifted Smitty six inches off the ground. With the blacksmith's hands still wrapped around his throat, Billy carried him to the forge and shoved him against it. The hot bed of coals burned through the back of the old man's shirt. He howled in pain and let go. Billy turned him and shoved him to the floor. Picking up tongs, the boy grabbed a red hot piece of iron. Straddling the old man, Billy held the glowing end near Smitty's face.

"Don't!" yelled Smitty, not daring to move.

"Now that I got your attention, old man," said Billy. "You tell these good folks how you're going to pay me a hundred dollars for four year's of work."

"Never!" spit out Smitty.

Billy moved his right arm and the tongs against Smitty's chest. The hot iron bit into the leather of his apron and Smitty howled again. Smoke rose up and the tip of glowing red went nearer to the man's face.

"Okay, okay!" yelled Smitty.

Billy stood up, threw the tongs and iron into the bed of coals, and looked at the crowd.

"You're all witnesses," said Billy. "Marshal, would you go see that Smitty does as promised?"

The marshal accompanied the blacksmith into his private rooms. When they returned, Smitty was spitting out words.

"I'll remember this, you Irish skunk."

"Not as long as I will, old man," responded Billy.

Smitty furiously counted out a hundred dollars in twenty dollar gold pieces into the boy's hand. The crowd applauded. Billy took the money and walked away from the blacksmith shop. After four years, there wasn't one item of his own to take with him.

"What are you going to do now, Billy?" asked the marshal.

"The foreman of the Double D offered me a job as a hand. He said if I showed up with my own outfit, he'd teach me to cowboy."

"Good plan, Billy. But a hundred dollars won't take you far."

"I got it worked out with the general store and the livery. They're selling me some clothes, tack, and a pony cheap. I should even have a little coin left over."

By the end of the day, the entire town showed up to see the young man in his new gear. Wearing new clothes, sombrero, boots, belt, and pistol, he looked mighty handsome on that black mustang. Not akin to demonstrative goodbyes, the westerners waved good luck as Billy O'Reilly rode out.

THE RAIN POURS ON

Clouds swept in and with them came pouring rain. Swirls of white descended to the ground in a gray fog that hung in the air and raindrops poured through it. The temperature dropped and cold mist and moisture penetrated the bones. Dreary weather was dampening to the spirit and ruined all plans for the day. Oldsters predicted a forty-eight hour continuation. The county would be blanketed with the front and it was either stay indoors or bundle up and endure the deluge.

Leonard bundled up. He was the youngest in the bunkhouse and the old dirty jobs fell to him. One thing worse than cleaning up horse manure, was cleaning it up wet. The new high-heeled boots the novice cowhand wore sunk deep into the mud, and the clay stuck to them. With each step the boots collected more, until there were great clots of it attached to the youth's feet.

"Tarnation, youngster!" shouted the foreman. "Forget the corral for today and clean up the stable!"

With difficulty Leonard walked out of the corral and into the barn. The boots collected more clay and made huge holes that quickly filled with water. Holes, the foreman noted, that would have to be filled in. With relief, the new hand got out of the rain, pulled off his slicker, shook it, and hung it up. He picked up the pitchfork and scraped the heavy mud off the bottom of his boots. Then he began cleaning the stalls.

"It works better," commented the foreman dryly. "If you take the horse out of the stall and put him in another before you start pitching that stuff."

Leonard had come from back east. It was his Uncle Russell's ranch. The foreman watched the boy for a while and then went back to his shack next to the bunkhouse.

"That kid," mumbled the foreman to himself. "He don't know one end of a horse from another."

Leonard worked hard and carted the manure to the end of the stable and piled it high. He figured that today was not the time to put it outside on the main pile. Taking straw, he distributed it loosely on the inside of the last stall, and he paused to wipe his forehead of moisture. He had cleaned ten enclosures for the mares. Uncle Russell was cross breeding horses as well as raising steers. The mares were nearly ready to foal and they needed to be kept out of the rain.

The kid sat down on a bench and stared out through an open door at the pouring rain. The corral, the surrounding yard, and the entire countryside were drenched. Leonard realized that all the land had turned to adobe clay, and that travel would be impossible. Just getting back to his bunk would be an ordeal and a muddy mess. Leonard decided to stay in the barn, rather then enter the smelly smoke-filled bunkhouse. The idea struck him that here would be a safer place to live. He would ask the foreman, and if he refused, his uncle, if he could sleep in the stable. If he cleaned up the tack room there would be plenty of space, a place with peace and quiet and away from the constant ribbing of the cowhands.

His uncle offered a bed in the house, but Leonard wanted to live with the hands. Uncle Russell told him that he would suffer. Leonard didn't know what a greenhorn was in for amongst the seasoned cowboys. Now he knew. Each day he must prove himself or face humiliation and ribbing. He couldn't give up and go back to the boss's house with his tail between his legs. He was determined to become a cowboy. Leonard was sticking it out, but he would do it his way. The tack room would be a suitable compromise.

The constant tomfoolery of the cowboys was hard to take. Their idea of fun wasn't his. Sometimes it just went too far. He didn't need a fangless rattlesnake in his bed, or scorpions without their stingers in his boots. But he did the jobs assigned to him, and performed them to the best of his abilities. Since his Ma passed, and he had no other place to go, he couldn't back down. He would show his uncle he could be as good a hand as any cowman on the place. But there was so much he had to learn and Leonard realized it would take years. They would have to drag him off in chains before he gave up trying.

The boy sat on the stool and stared out the open door through the mist and constant drizzle. What bothered him the most was that no matter how hard he tried, he was always doing something wrong. The foreman was on him and so were the cowhands. They laughed at him and played tricks every moment. It was a hard school and so far he was flunking.

The rain lasted two full days. The sun came out and burned off the water and dried the mud. By the fourth day, only the lowest spots contained the sticky clay, and the rest of the land baked as hard as rock. The ponds were now full and grass, some of it lying dormant for years, sprung up and turned the countryside a luscious green. In the dry prairie it was an awesome sight. It wouldn't be long before the sun turned it straw yellow.

Leonard learned that each day on the Colorado Front Range brought different views. He had seen the land dry up and turn to beige, bare ground that looked like it was good for nothing except for the harsh winds to blow away. The dirt would have, if the sun hadn't baked it. Spring was his favorite time of year. Everything turned green and cactus of every color bloomed. It contrasted with mountains that rose high in the blue sky. Snow blanketed their peaks. Leonard never tired of the changing scenery.

When his chores were done for the day and with permission not of the foreman but of his uncle, Leonard cleaned up the tack room. For the first time since the ranch was built, the tack was put in order. All the bridles were hung neatly along the wall and the saddles stored on saddle trees. What pegs or trees there was a shortage of, Leonard made. He was skilled with his hands and did a good job. His bunk he enclosed with a wall of lumber. He would not make it easy for the cowhands to enter his private domain. This was a small triumph against the foreman and hands on the ranch. It made it all the more satisfactory to the boy.

Leonard sat down to dinner in the cook shack. His uncle commented on the neatness of the tack room, and told the boy it was time he learned to mend the leather as well. The youth wasn't sure if this was a promotion or another dirty job. He thought about it and decided he would like to work with the tack.

Leonard should have known something was up. His plate was filled and one of the hands passed it down, along with black coffee. One spoonful told him it was full of salt. Eyes beamed as the boy chewed. Mouths were covered and the men refused to look his way. Leonard ate slowly and swallowed. He looked at his uncle and saw an expression of keen observation. The boy gritted his teeth and ate every bite of his meal. He followed with the coffee, also spiked with salt. Every day was like this, an endless succession of foolish pranks. Finished, Leonard got up nonchalantly and commented to Cookie on the way out.

"Good chuck!"

He walked across the yard. Behind the stable he rushed to a pump and trough and quickly worked the handle. He stuck his head under and cleared his mouth and throat with cold water.

"Maybe you boys should ease up on the lad," expressed the rancher inside the cook shack. "You don't need to bust him down to nothing."

"Awe, boss," said the foreman. "Yeah coddle him by letting him sleep in the tack room."

"The lad's showing spunk," the owner said. "You just let him have his privacy."

The other cowhands looked disappointed that they lost some control over their latest source of amusement.

Leonard was given his own horse and it was on this wiry mustang that he learned to ride. After supper it was his habit to get in a few hours. If he were to become a hand, and survive all the dirty jobs on the ranch, he needed to learn on his own. His uncle also gave him a pistol and rifle. Leonard would travel miles away from the ranch and practice shooting. With the rifle, he quickly became a good shot. The pistol was another matter. One evening he spotted a mule deer and brought it down with one shot. His uncle welcomed fresh venison, and Leonard brought it to the cook shack for Cookie to dispose of.

The sun had set. The boy made his way to the tack room, lit a lantern, hung up his rifle, pistol belt, and sombrero. He sat on the bed and it collapsed with a bang. He rose from the floor and examined the supports. They were sawn through. He thought he heard laughter and receding footsteps. This was a last straw. Leonard resolved that in some way, he would get even. It was well past the time that they show him a modicum of respect and that these silly pranks end.

It was late before Leonard finished considering all the possible plans his imagination could think up. He finally settled on one and went to sleep. In the morning he worked hard at all his assigned chores, and took without complaint the extra ones that the foreman ordered. The young man showed a better humor and increased enthusiasm. The cowboys and the foreman noticed and wondered.

Leonard worked at his prank whenever the hands were absent. It would take a long time to complete the work, and he was careful that his uncle and Cookie didn't catch him. He needed block and tackle and extra rope. These items the youth purchased on his own and carefully hid. It took weeks to methodically detach the supports holding the object of his prank together. When he was finished, he climbed up a large cottonwood, whose limbs would make the joke possible. Now all that was needed was a good heavy rain.

On the Colorado grassland, below the Rocky Mountains, rain is very unpredictable. It is even possible that rain wouldn't come at all. Drought on the desert prairie was common. Rain clouds could pass overhead and not leave a drop. A single cloud could dump buckets in one small area and dissipate, leaving the rest of the prairie dry. Most often, rain came only three or four times a year. It could be anything from a light sprinkle, to hail, or a deluge that swept down mountainsides and through arroyos carrying tons of rocks and earth, transforming the landscape with its raging power.

Days and months passed. Leonard realized the pranks were lessoning. The hard work the youth performed without complaint was gaining the cowboys' respect. As the youth showed better humor and took the many jokes played on him in a manly manner, they grudgingly began to believe the lad would make a hand. Some of the cowboys started to befriend the young man. One taught him roping, another how to shoot his pistol. When roundup came in the fall, Leonard was invited by his uncle to participate.

After the hard work of branding cattle, the men returned tired to the bunkhouse. They were all looking for their monthly pay, and a weekend visit to town. It was on that Thursday night that the wind blew and clouds gathered. Leonard was not sure now that he should carry out his massive prank. He vacillated. Just when he thought things were going well, the men again salted his food and sawed his bed.

That night the rain began to fall, it came on hard and beat down in torrents. In the middle of this storm Leonard climbed the tree and attached blocks to two limbs. Then he suspended thick ropes. He tied them to the proper corners. Hitching a team to a wagon, already in position, he climbed up and released the brake. The horses, uncomfortable in the downpour, pulled hard. The roof of the bunkhouse cracked and rose up in the air.

The shouts of outrage came loudly through the noise of the steady rain. Thunder sounded and lightning flashed. The rain increased and so did the complaints from the cowboys within. Leonard had trouble holding the horses and it was only possible by using the brake. When the lad thought the cowboys had enough, he lowered the roof back down. It settled crookedly onto the building. As some of the men came out in the rain to investigate what had caused the roof to move, a flash of lightning revealed Leonard leading a team of horses into the barn.

"It's Leonard!" shouted one of the cowboys. "Dang my hide, but that boy done this here job!"

The bellowing came frequent and loud. Lanterns began to illuminate part of the night. A light came on in the foreman's quarters and Uncle Russell's house. Leonard anticipated the commotion and, having his mustang saddled, rode off into the dark to escape the cowboys' wrath. He already planned to spend the rest of the night in a broken down shack. The roof he had carefully repaired for this event. For several hours the ranch hands looked for Leonard but could not locate him.

"Well," said the uncle. "You men done messed with my nephew and yeah all got it back good."

The next day, after the roof was squared and nailed back down, the cowboys laid out their gear to dry. Discussion was generally that once the incident was examined by the light of day, the lad had pulled off the biggest prank of all. The men went off to guard the herd, and ride the fence line. In their absence, Leonard came back to do his work and hoped he would survive the cowhands' wrath. That evening, at the cook shack, the men guffawed, slapped the youngster on the back, and welcomed him without reservation.

"Boss," said the foreman. "I reckon its time we start rotatin the stable job. Looks like tomorrow I'm makin Leonard a full hand."

SOMETHING IN THE WOODPILE

"Well, consarnit, you old fool," snarled Art. "You going to play or not?"

"No! Who wants to play with an old buzzard who insults a man every time he wants his own way?"

Two old geezers sat at a rough table in their homemade chairs while the single kerosene lantern swung above them. Nearby stood a cook stove, hot with fire, their only source of heat in the tiny one room cabin. A cold wind blew outside and filtered in between cracks in the flimsy wooden walls. Zeke sat puffing on a corncob pipe and reading from an old yellow-paged book. Art, on the other side, stared idly and shoved checkers around a wooden red and black checker board.

"Haw, haw!" retorted Art. "You ain't been a man since you were spry enough to fit in that War Between the States."

"If that's the case, you dried up carcass, then you ain't no man neither. Not since you shot the first buffalo and trapped the last beaver."

Art and Zeke were like that, two old coots who found each other in their final years. They shared poverty on a little homestead near the tiny western town of Walsenburg,

Colorado. They were frontiersmen who outlived the wild days when white men were scarce in the west and Indians and buffalo roamed free.

* * *

It was an old and wily packrat that came to the top of the hill. Staying hidden from the hawks and owls, it climbed up on a mound. Surrounded by thick pins-and-needle grass, it looked down at the valley below. There stood a wooden cabin, a crooked little stable, corrals, and a couple old horses. Smoke was rising from a bent chimney on the dilapidated cabin, and nearby was a large woodpile of cut piñon and cedar.

Where there were humans there was food, and where there was a woodpile there was shelter. Humans also had shiny things, and being a consummate collector and hoarder of such items, the packrat scurried along through the dense cover down to the cabin. It found the woodpile and explored it. Finding an opening in the back and a likely place to set up residence, the packrat began gathering grass and bits of spiny cactus to line and protect its new home.

After exploring the entire region around its shelter, the packrat set to chewing through a feed bag and eating some of the oats for the horses. Here appeared a never ending source of food. Also, there was dripping water from a pump and trough. Delicious smells emanated from the cabin. Searching along the foundation, a crack was found, and with some judicious chewing, the fourteen inch packrat was able to find its way in. Two separate, loud, staccato snores, whistles, and sputtering noises came from opposite corners of the cabin. The packrat listened briefly, and then went about his business.

The little hoarder explored the cabin. It found a gleaming coin which it discarded for a small pin knife, which in turn it dropped for a gold nugget. The nugget was quickly left in an ashtray on top of a dresser in exchange for a shiny silver pocket watch. This it carried in its mouth. The creature climbed around clutter and made its way outside and to the nest. The little fellow was very pleased with the new addition. Each time the packrat looked, it was startled and delighted by seeing its tiny face in the shiny surface of the watch.

"What's going on around here!" shouted Art.

Zeke awoke from his sputtering and sat upright, startled by his partner's loud voice.

"What's eatin you? You howl like a coyote. That's no way to wake a man."

"Looky here! My watch is stolen!"

"I didn't take it!"

"Well, someone did! If I don't get it back, there's going to be a shootin!"

From that moment on, the rough good natured harmony of the two old frontiersmen ended. Art began to tear apart the cabin, piece by piece, looking for his watch. When the contents of the room were completely turned upside down and the watch remained missing, Art became ornery and mean as an old bear.

"My pappy gave me that there watch! If I don't find it, there's going to be heck to pay."

As he said this, Art sat at the table. He had before him

an old Walker Colt, and he loaded its cylinders with lead and powder. He applied explosive caps to the nipples of the ancient pistol.

"You old fool," commented Zeke. "You try to fire that thing and it'll tear off your arm and knock you to kingdom come."

"Oh Yeah?" commented Art, glaring menacingly at his one time friend and companion.

The next night the packrat made two visits to the cabin and carried away the gold nugget and the pin knife, both of which belonged to old Zeke. In the morning the two men argued.

"Just cause you lost your pocket watch doesn't mean you had to steal my lucky nugget and my tobaccy knife," shouted Zeke.

"Balderdash! I ain't never stole nothing in my life!"

"Rubbish! You stole them sure as I'm standing here!"

"Take that back, you old coot!" shouted Art reaching for his pistol.

The two men fought over the ancient weapon. Zeke gave Art a mighty shove. He dropped with a weighty crash and cracked his head against the heavy iron cook stove. As Art fell, the .44 Walker Colt discharged with a mighty blast.

The packrat remained until all the oats were eaten. This was speeded along by the two old mustangs breaking down their corral and helping themselves to the bags of meal. When the food was gone, and the smell from the silent cabin began to dissipate, the packrat decided it was time to move on. It traveled by night and a great distance.

When it finally climbed another large hill many days later, the packrat looked down on a neat little farm, with a barn, two story cabin, corrals, horses, cows, and pigs. Here was another place with a long high woodpile and it was sheltered by an overhang next to the large cabin itself. With alacrity, the packrat descended to its new home.

As before, it found a likely hole and lined the inner home with grass and protected it with spines of cactus. It began to explore that night and found, dropped from a laundry line, a pair of delicate female panties. This soft material it took back to the inner sanctum of its home. The garment smelled fresh and clean, and was wonderfully pleasant to lie on. Exploring further, the packrat found meal in the large barn and bit through burlap to get at the oats.

The next morning, Sally complained to her mother that Toby, her nasty little brother, had stolen her undergarment. Her favorite, the one that came from Sears & Roebuck, all the way from Chicago.

"I didn't steal it," complained Toby when confronted.

"You did too!" shouted back the angry sister.

Harmony on the Stevens' ranch was broken. The next night the packrat explored inside the house and found, tucked in the back corner of Mr. Stevens' bedroom, a leather pouch. It was half open and inside were three shiny silver dollars. The pouch was carried back to the nest.

"Someone stole the money I was saving for mother's birthday dress," complained Mr. Stevens. "Three whole dollars! Now I want to know which one of you took it!"

It was suppertime and sixteen-year-old Sally and

twelve-year-old Toby stood in front of their father near the dinner table. Both shook in fury at the astounding accusation.

"Father!" shouted Sally as she began to cry.

She ran to her bedroom door and slammed it shut without having supper.

"I didn't take it!" protested Toby with hot tears in his eyes.

"Go to your bed!" shouted the angry father.

Toby climbed the ladder to the loft. Going to bed with hunger pains in his stomach, made the false accusation all the worse.

"Glenn Stevens!" commented his wife, Helen. "How can you accuse our own children of such a thing?"

"Well, who else would take it?"

The next night the very plump packrat made another excursion to the barn for a quick meal and then scampered inside the house. There he found a shiny silver watch; this was small and easy to carry.

"Good heavens!" declared Helen Stevens loudly the next morning. "My brooch-pin watch is gone."

Everyone awakened early and all four of the Stevens searched the house, looking for the little silver watch. When they didn't find it the first time, they looked again. They moved every item in the house and searched very carefully. Still it was not found.

"Oh," cried Mrs. Stevens, obviously very upset. "Who could do such a thing? That was the watch Grandmamma gave to me."

The atmosphere of the Stevens' home was greatly

upset. No one was talking to anyone, and suspicion hung heavily in the air. The next morning they all got up silently, dressed in their Sunday best, and took the work wagon to church. That night they had a quiet supper, and everyone was too upset to clear away the table or do the dishes. That night it rained, and there was a drip, drip, drip of water in a corner of the parent's bedroom.

"I told you to get that leak fixed," complained the wife coldly to her husband.

Before breakfast, the mother carried wet items out to the clothesline to dry. Among them was Mr. Stevens' new Sunday hat, and Mrs. Stevens' new Sunday dress. One she had spent many hours cutting and sewing from an expensive bolt of cloth.

The smell of last night's supper reached the furry packrat. The remains still lay on dirty dishes at the kitchen table. It was too much for the hungry creature. Throwing away instinct and caution the packrat climbed up on the table and began chewing. Toby, bleary eyed, looked down from his perch in the loft and saw the big rodent with its nine inch tufted-tail—chewing away in delight. Mrs. Stevens, returning with a straw clothes basket from outside saw the hairy creature at the same time.

"Glenn!" screamed Helen Stevens in a stentorian voice. "There's a rat on our table!"

"It's a packrat!" corrected Toby.

There was crashing in the far bedroom. Mr. Stevens, dressed in long johns, came rushing out with a loaded shotgun. The packrat, bolted off the table, ran out the door, and headed towards the clothesline. Mr. Stevens ran outside in his bare feet. He saw the rodent running away. The father was never much with a shotgun. He pointed the barrel at the packrat, and hurriedly pulled the trigger. The heavy buckshot pellets perforated his new Sunday-go-to-meeting hat. Pulling back the second hammer of the shotgun, Mr. Stevens carefully raised and aimed again. He took a bead on the disappearing rodent. The weapon fired and blew an oval circle out of Mrs. Stevens' dress.

"You fool!" shouted Helen Stevens at her husband.

Toby and Sally stood at the kitchen door. They had seen the inexpert marksmanship and watched the packrat escape unharmed. They both grinned and looked at each other.

"Well," said Toby. "I reckon that explains the missing items."

"Yes," laughed Sally. "And Mama is sure going to need that new dress now."

ON THE EDGE

I hung to the edge of the cliff; the tips of my fingers clutching a ledge of solid granite rock. My arms stretched taut, and my feet dangled uselessly finding no outcropping on the smooth rock. I tried to balance myself and looked down. It was a drop of more than six hundred feet. I whistled to my horse and he whinnied above me. I looked up and there he was looking down, his dangling reins too far away to reach. If I was going to get out of this predicament, I had to do it myself.

It was my own fault. Blacky, my mustang gelding, tried to warn me not to advance up the steep trail. He fought the reins. I got angry and spurred him. He reared up when the coiled rattlesnake struck at his legs. I went over the saddle, hit the trail on my back, and rolled off the edge of the cliff. On the way down, my feet hit a lip of rock, the soles slipped along with my body, and I managed to grab hold with my hands. They stung pretty bad and there was torn skin.

Above me my horse neighed. Good old Blacky. He would help if he could. If I was going to have a chance to get out of this I'd better, "do something, even if it's wrong." An expression my dad always used on me. Dear old dad, dead and gone now. He had set in that rocking chair on the porch to his last dying breath, telling all those hair-raising stories. Not one of them came close to this one. What would he do?

I lifted a hand from the ledge and slapped it back down several inches to my right. My body weight pulled when I did. I nearly lost hold. I needed to slide my hands along the wall and continue until I found some outcropping that would allow me to climb with both feet and hands. But the rock below me was as smooth as a baby's bottom.

Good thing my son's not here. He always likes to ride ahead of me. His foolish pony might have jumped off the cliff to avoid the snake. Then how could I live with myself? Still, this is a mighty foolish situation for a grown man to find himself in. I've got to get back up that cliff. How will my wife and son run the ranch without me? They'd lose it, starve, or get run off. That three-hundred twenty acre spread has a crick and spring. More than most ranches have in this dry Colorado country. There's many a rancher who'd go after it, knowing I was gone.

I thought of my wife's sky-blue eyes and fine figure and my boy's mischievous freckled grin and corn-shock hair.

With renewed vigor, I pulled myself along with my finger tips. Again I nearly lost hold. If only I was wearing gloves. No, I needed to feel the rock with my bare skin; I might slide off with gloves on. My fingers were bleeding now, rubbed raw. Despite the pain, I slid my right hand and then my left along the cliff edge. I kept searching for a hold with my boots. Then, my right toe caught on a lip of rock. I tested it cautiously and then added more weight. This gave me temporary relief from the strain on my fingers. I rested a moment and regained some strength. Taking a deep breath, I continued sliding to the right. This time it was easier, as I balanced my weight with the toe of my right boot.

I felt the sun move in the cloudless sky. It passed an outcropping of mountain rock and began shining directly down on me, a man who foolishly clung to a solid wall of granite by his finger tips. Above, a buzzard drifted with extended dark wings. It caught hidden winds and sailed on past. I know, because I saw its shadow and wasted precious energy looking up. It stared back and I am sure it wondered.

Inching on, my toe hold was lost. Again I hung suspended by fingertips. Moisture poured from me and my clothing was drenched. Worse, sweat poured into my eyes and it stung. I would give anything to be able to pause and wipe them clear. Strength faltered, and my breath came in great gasps. I had no choice but to continue on lacerated fingers as I slid them along the rough rock. Again I found toe holds for both my boots. I rested. Another few moments, and I surely would have lost my grip.

I thought of my wife, my son, and my ranch. Strangely, in my mind, I went over this week's work. It was a habit of mine to write down my weekly chores. I took pleasure in crossing out each item completed. It was my way of knowing I had accomplished something—that time spent was not wasted. It was a task I was teaching my son. These idle thoughts filled my mind as I worked my way along the cliff. I must think of something, anything, to ease the strain and pain of holding on. I could not fall; I would not give up. My family needed me. "Please God! Just help me out of this," I prayed.

I lost purchase with my feet again. My right hand slipped, and I hung there by my left. My toes, looking for a hold, found none. This time I would fall. In panic, I stretched my right foot further out along the wall. It touched a ledge! My whole foot came down and rested on it. I pushed up and grabbed with my right hand and then quickly with my left. I moved farther to the right and both hands and feet now had solid holds and rested firmly on rock. I could rest now. Balancing against the granite wall, standing on my two feet, I let go with my hands. I wiped the sweat from my forehead and eyes with my shirt sleeve. Relief!

I balanced there, with my arms down by my side. Blood rushed back into them. My racing heart slowed, and my energy began to return. I looked up, and saw Blacky with his head still hanging over the cliff.

"Hold on, Blacky!" I called with renewed confidence. "I'll climb up there in a moment."

My horse neighed. I looked to my right and I saw, some twenty feet away, a fissure. It looked like it was a few inches wide and near the ledge I was standing on. From there it went straight up the cliff. At the top, near the trail, it opened up. With new hope, I placed my hands against the rock wall, and slid my feet along the ledge. I balanced myself carefully and in a few minutes came to the crack.

I jammed a fist into the fissure above me and tried to

pull my weight up. My hand held firm. I let myself back down on the ledge, rested a few minutes, and then started again. I placed a closed fist into the opening, pulled my body up, while using the toes of my boots to push. I worked my way up slowly. With the exertion, the sweat returned, and my heart raced. I concentrated on what I was doing and did not look up or down. Several times a hand, or a boot, got stuck in the crack. I would get a good hold with the opposite hand or foot, and work the other loose and continue up.

I was so busy concentrating on the climb that when I came to the ledge of the upper trail, I was surprised. With a final effort, I clawed my way up and over onto the five foot trail. I rested flat on my back. It was an awesome relief. I caught my breath and could hardly believe I was alive. Then there was Blacky's soft muzzle in my face. I laughed. Caressing his soft snout, I reached up for his bridle and pulled myself to my feet. I felt dizzy and totally drained.

"Well boy," I said out loud. "With God's help, we made it!"

DEAD MAN'S SONG

As he lay up in the jumble of rocks against Badito Cone, Bobby Carter knew he was a dead man. The Indians surrounded him. Four hours before, in the early dawn, he had broken camp and followed the Huerfano River south. He was only three miles from the village of Badito when Tierra Blanca and his small band of Ute warriors jumped him and chased him into the canyon.

Arrows flew in a storm and showered down on the white man among the rocks. Bobby hunkered behind and underneath a hanging boulder as big as a house. The arrows hit and shattered without striking him—but they were close, so very close. Bobby Carter hummed a tune under his breath, as he had since childhood. Always there were songs and melodies in his head.

Tierra Blanca fumed. There were so many whites coming into their lands; if they were not stopped, they would take everything. Already the game was scarce. That white village on the Huerfano was growing larger. Those intruders took over the land and defended it with their steel guns. They had no right. This was Ute land and the time was long past to fight and wipe the invaders out.

The man in the rocks was traveling alone. They had his horse and now he had no way out. He would die, but it would not be easy to take his life. He had guns, and in the rocks, there was safety from their bows. Thirst and starvation would weaken him, but that would take time. White men might come from the village to see what the shooting was about. They could come in large numbers and more warriors would be lost.

Is it worth it? thought Chief Blanca. *Is this one white man worth the wait and risk of facing so many others with their accurate weapons?*

From high in the rocks came a peculiar sound—the ringing of a musical chord. It was a guitar, the same as the Spanish played. And, with the strumming came a clear tenor voice raised in song. Many of the Utes had learned the English tongue—some taught by mountain men, others by whites who came among them. The warriors listened to the voice and the guitar. The music was strange, but pleasant. It carried clearly through the dry air.

It rained all night the day I left, the weather it was dry. Sun so hot nearly froze to death, Susannah don't you cry...

The song continued. Despite himself, Chief Tierra Blanca smiled. This was a brave man. In all the battles he had fought, never had a foe lifted a voice in joy or happiness. The only song he ever heard a man sing was his death chant. This was not that kind of melody. It was clearly a song of gaiety.

The Utes put down their bows and listened. Here was a strange enemy, one to be respected. There were not many men, White or Indian, who could sing and make joy in the face of death.

Eventually the song ended and there was quiet. But the hearts of all the warriors were changed towards this lone white man. Even Chief Blanca sat idly and wondered. The morning passed to midday and all was silent. The intruder had no water and in the rays of the sun, the rocks would heat up. This white would become thirsty and suffer. There would be no more singing.

Chief Blanca ordered two braves to move forward. When the Utes briefly showed themselves, the man shot with his pistol. One warrior came back with a wound in his arm. The other returned to tell his chief that the singing man was well protected in the rocks and, from his position, could defend all directions.

The wait continued through the hot day and into the afternoon. When it turned cooler, the white man called out.

"Hey, you Utes! How about another song?"

The guitar echoed down again. The chords sounded clear and melodious. The man sang from his heart and he had a soothing quality in his voice, despite his dry throat.

The years creep slowly by, Lorena, the snow is on the grass again; the sun's low down the sky, Lorena, the frost gleams where the flowers have been; but the heart throbs on as lovely now, as when the days were nigh...

Again the Ute warriors put down their bows and sat among the rocks to listen. The white man finished his song and quickly went into the lilting refrain of *The Yellow Rose of Texas*. Chief Blanca leaned his back against a stone in what shade he could find. The Ute chief looked around at his warriors who sat listening to this man sing. He became angry and barked out orders to attack.

Pistol fire answered the deluge of arrows. The running warriors were stopped before they started. Two came back with dripping wounds to be bandaged.

"Now for your listening pleasure," called out the white man. "I would like to sing *Oh, Hard Times Come Again No More*. If you know it, join in."

Let us pause in life's pleasures and count its many tears, while we all sup sorrow with the poor, there's a song that will linger forever in our ears, oh hard times come again no more...

Chief Blanca heard humming and turned to see one of his warriors actually trying to imitate the melody of the song.

How can we kill a man such as this? wondered the chief.

Despite himself, the Ute gave a begrudging smile in recognition of this man's courage. In answer to his quick signal, the warriors backed away from the ambush and went for their mustangs. The chief motioned to leave the horse of their foe. In a moment the warriors were mounted. In the clear dry air as they rode away, they heard the second refrain of the song.

Tis the song, the sigh of the weary, hard times, hard times, come again no more, many days you have lingered around my cabin door; oh hard times come again no more...

Bobby Carter sang with conviction. He knew that before nightfall he would be dead and lying among the rocks. All his life he had loved music, even in times of trouble. He carried his guitar with him everywhere; it was how he made his living. Bobby was greatly surprised when near the end of the song he heard the hoofs of the Indian ponies beat loudly and then fade into the distance. Despite the welcoming sound, Bobby kept playing and singing. Through dry mouth and rasping throat, he gave it his all. For never in his life had he ever quit in the middle of a performance.

ACKNOWLEDGEMENTS

ROPE AND WIRE

Publisher and Editor, Scott Gese

This publication is far, far more than an on-line magazine. It is as it claims, a total Western Community. The Western enthusiast can watch cowboy movies, listen to old time radio shows, find chuck wagon recipes, book reviews, and read excellent Western fiction and Cowboy Poetry. This site has something to interest everyone. (www.ropeandwire.com)

**Grandma Gives no Quarter,* 1st printing, July 2008

**Old Man in a Rocking Chair,* 1st printing, August 2008

STORYTELLER, Canada's Short Story Magazine

Publisher, Terry Tyo

Editor, Melanie Fogel

The magazine was launched in 1994 and ended publication in 2008. The goal was to give Canadian writers an avenue to see their work in print and readers a place to access Canadian fiction. Fortunately, the goal expanded to include non-Canadian authors and readers. **STORYTELLER, Canada's Short Story Magazine** will be missed.

**The Lad from Norway,* 1st printing, Vol. 13/Issue 4, 2007

The LAKESHORE GUARDIAN

Publisher and Editor, Julie Purdy

Assistant Editor, Janis Stein

In 1999, **The LAKESHORE GUARDIAN** was created to connect the shoreline residents of the 'Thumb' area of Michigan. The paper, available also on-line, became a source of current concerns and events, as well as heart-warming nostalgia. It is an amazing chronicle of the Great Lakes and Michigan history. (www.lakeshoreguardian.com)

**Kid on the Run,* 1st printing, June/August 2006

**Little Sammy Tucker and the Strangers,* 1st printing, September 2007

The SHOOTIST

Editor, George Warnick

This magazine, now in its tenth year of publication, is the official magazine of the National Congress of Old West Shootists. **The SHOOTIST** not only provides up-to-date news and information about Western Action Shooting for its membership, but it includes interesting articles, book reviews, and prints Old West Fiction. (www.ncows.com)

**Desert Heat, Desert Cold,* 1st printing, September/ October 2007

**Boy on the Desert,* 1st printing, July/August 2007

**Death Comes in the Afternoon,* 1st printing, November/ December 2007

**The Dust Still Rising,* 1st printing, May/June 2007

Dear Reader,

If you enjoyed reading *Desert Heat, Desert Cold and Other Tales of the West, please help promote it by composing and posting a review on Amazon.com.*

Charlie Steel may be contacted at cowboytales@juno.com or by writing to him at the following address:

Charlie Steel
c/o Condor Publishing, Inc.
PO Box 39
Lincoln, Michigan 48742

Warm greetings from Condor Publishing, Inc.
Gail Heath, publisher

Lightning Source UK Ltd.
Milton Keynes UK
UKHW010636010621
384684UK00001BA/50